SAVING LEO KLEINMAN

A JERZY SHORE NOVEL

SAVING LEO KLEINMAN

A JERZY SHORE NOVEL

George Vercessi

EP
Edenton Press

ISBN: 0-9705014-1-2
ISBN-13: 978-0-9705014-1-7

Edenton Press, Alexandria, VA

Cover design by Melanie Stephens

Also by George Vercessi

NCIS Agent Jerzy Shore
King of the Hill
Alma's World
SEAL~Test
We the People
FREDO: A Christmas Tale

(Visit www.vercessi.com for details.)

To Lisa, John and Andrea, my wonderful children.
Love, Dad

Beware the fury of a patient adversary.
Publilius Syrus (b. 85 BC)

DISCLAIMER

With the exception of the June 8, 1967, assault on USS *Liberty*, which, in fact, did occur, the characters and events depicted in this story are entirely fictional. Any resemblance to actual persons, living or dead, is purely coincidental.

ONE

Laura Greene, forty-two, slight of build and currently unmarried, gulped the last of her wine, crushed out her cigarette, and pressed PRINT. Then, lacking energy to move away from her computer, she remained stoop-shouldered staring at the screen while the printer rumbled to life and spat out her latest rant to Leo Kleinman. Craving sleep, but fearing the recurring dreams that would surely jar her awake, she willed herself up and forced herself to perform unnecessary housekeeping tasks in one last attempt to delay heading off to bed.

When she could no longer continue, she placed her cigarettes on the kitchen counter beside the rear door, to be claimed later in the likelihood she'd need them, sighed, and trudged upstairs with little enthusiasm, while praying for just one night of uninterrupted sleep.

As before, her prayers went unanswered, and sometime in the early hours she was once again aboard the American spy ship, USS *Liberty*, plying the sun-drenched international waters of the eastern Mediterranean, off the coast of the sparsely populated Sinai Peninsula, this second day of what would later be termed the Six-Day War. The scene never varied, nor the events that followed. The sea was calm, no other ships in sight, and on the main deck sailors were sunbathing on steel beach. "It was just before all hell broke loose," as her now-deceased uncle had so often described it.

In the next instant, her body tensed at the sound of the pulsating klaxon followed by the boatswain's shrill voice.

This is not a drill. This is not a drill. General quarters. General quarters. All hands man your battle stations. The ship is under attack.

And so began the all-too familiar nightmare that denied her needed sleep these many months. She saw the sunbathers rushing to don life jackets and helmets, most barely reaching their battle stations as the first wave of Israeli jets crisscrossing overhead delivered an unrelenting, ear-shattering stream of rocket and cannon fire into the defenseless ship.

She saw steel bulkheads buckle like cardboard, and white-hot steel fragments and shrapnel cut men down in midstride, strewing bloody body parts across the gray deck. She heard screams emerge from clouds of dense smoke and saw an officer on the bridge slammed against the deck, his mangled leg twisted beneath him and a wide blood stain blossoming across his starched khaki shirt. She saw shrapnel catch the young helmsman at the base of his skull, and watched his lifeless body crumple. She saw radiomen in the comms shack aft of the bridge doused in a shower of sparks from severed high-voltage wires, the air filling with the pungent odor of ozone, as precisely aimed gunfire disabled the forest of antennas on the deck above them, effectively silencing all calls for help.

Her breathing grew shallow and sweat covered her, but there was no escaping the images of men below decks—boys, really. The average age of the crew being twenty—slipping in pools of blood and oil from ruptured lines while scurrying for cover.

Her body shuddered as machine gun fire cut through the ship's hull puncturing fire hoses and wreaking havoc in cramped passageways, where stretcher-bearers dropped to the deck with each new explosion, sending their wounded charges tumbling. She saw one sailor attempt to hoist an injured buddy through a hatch and recoil when the man's arm came away in his grip.

She saw the executive officer sprinting toward burning fuel drums to release them into the sea before they exploded, and the rocket striking nearby liquefying his legs.

The nightmare continued when a second sortie unleashed canisters of napalm sending walls of flames from the main deck up four levels to the bridge, the jellied gasoline coating every surface and surging through rocket holes to sear crewmen inside.

It was usually at this point Laura bolted upright, as she did now, soaked in sweat and struggling to breathe. Sitting there in the dark of night on the edge of her bed, she began steadying her pulse with rhythmic breathing as she'd been counseled, a technique that failed as often as it worked. Regardless, the result was always the same, she'd eventually settle back into her pillow wide awake and exhausted.

"Recurring dreams and visions usually mean there's something in your life you haven't acknowledged or resolved that's causing you stress," her analyst had informed her when she sought treatment nearly a year earlier. "The dream or vision repeats because you haven't corrected the problem."

Which problem would that be? She'd had a lifetime of problems caring for her disabled uncle and his alcoholic wife. Now, with both dead, she was embarked on a course to resolve the problem she believed was the source of her anxiety, which is what brought her here, to Butner, North Carolina.

Laura dragged herself from bed, put on her robe, and headed for her cigarettes and a dose of fresh night air. Absent city lights, the sky was bright with stars and the night quiet except for an occasional semi on nearby Interstate 85 and the rustle of trees from a random breeze. With the neighbors' houses dark—folks turned in early in these parts—she had the night to herself.

She lit her cigarette with trembling hands and held the smoke long and deep while surveying the heavens, but the tranquil scene did little to calm her. The frequency and intensity of her dreams, surfacing as they did with unnerving regularity, caused her to question her sanity and left her pacing the deck in tight circles and chain-smoking her way through several cigarettes. When she was done, she headed inside and returned to bed, where she reluctantly closed her eyes, hoping for a few hours of undisturbed sleep before the sun arose.

Three motor-torpedo boats appeared on the horizon and the words every seaman fears rang in her ears: *Stand by for torpedo attack starboard side.*

The chief engineer's order to "Evacuate the engine room!" sent a knot of sailors scrambling up steep ladders to escape what would be certain death. Behind them, the chief engineer and several volunteers stood fast, ready to answer the bridge's engine orders that would keep the ship on an evasive course should the engine room be spared. Several decks above, men rushing to carry the wounded to the port side were tripping over twisted lengths of fire hoses rendered useless by machine gun bullets.

"Please, God, let me go home," a seaman cried out, his young voice lost in the confusion.

The scene was calmer in the ship's cryptologist spaces three decks below the waterline, where the embarked crypto team, lacking assigned battle stations, remained in place. Those not busy preparing classified material for destruction were seated on the deck, bracing their backs against the bulkheads.

Laura shivered when the torpedo armed with a thousand pounds of high-energy explosives struck, disintegrating bulkheads and sending typewriters and other loose gear through the air with the deadly force of missiles. She'd heard stories of men blinded by flying paint chips, of shattered eardrums, and bodies torn apart as a forty-foot hole opened to the sea, instantly killing twenty-five men.

Survivors found themselves chin-deep in rising water in pitch-dark spaces no longer familiar to them. A dim light from an open watertight hatch beckoned, but reaching it before the flooding sea forced shipmates above to secure it proved difficult, if not impossible. The blast had dramatically altered the landscape, forcing survivors to navigate a maze of jagged, ruptured pipes, exposed cables, upturned furniture and the mutilated bodies of shipmates.

The carnage on the bridge a hundred feet above was no less gruesome, where mangled bodies lay beside the badly wounded, and the commanding officer clung to the railing praying his beloved ship would not capsize and sink as the Israelis intended.

Laura watched the *Liberty* roll hard to port while all aboard prayed. At the point it appeared she was about to go under, the ship slowly began righting herself.

She awakened at the sound of her alarm, drained of all energy.

TWO

I strolled into the room and immediately sized up the competition. This was my fifth speed dating gig in as many months and I was now comfortable with the routine. I had been uncertain at first, wondering if I was meant for this urban sport, but with romance eluding me, I eventually decided to test the waters. That was several months ago and, while I've met many women since then, I was still searching for the right one.

With each event, I picked up new pointers about today's dating scene, like business casual among the younger crowd isn't what it used to be. Sport jackets and ties were verboten, and clearly a turnoff for the ladies. It was now jeans and Polo shirts, a line I hadn't yet crossed and likely wouldn't. But I did discard the jacket and tie. I also learned to adapt to new venues, like vape lounges and hookah bars, neither of which appealed to me.

In keeping with this evening's Polynesian theme, I wore my Tommy Bahama flowered shirt and a puka necklace with a dangling shark tooth I had picked up in Hawaii. I knew it was a bit over the top, but figured what's life without a few laughs.

I arrived around seven, slapped on my *Aloha, my name is Jerzy* name tag and, after surveying the room and deciding the thirty dollars admission looked to be well spent, ordered a mai tai.

"Hold the pink umbrella," I told the young bartender, whose shirt matched mine.

"Here you go, pal," he said when delivering my drink. Offering a wink and a grin, he said, "You're gonna knock 'em dead with that necklace. Puts this to shame," he said fingering his pink and yellow paper lei.

"Think so?" I said, enjoying his humor.

"Can't miss."

The room continued to fill with women about fifteen years younger than the men. And while I wasn't the only fifty-plus guy there, I was pleased to see from my perch at the bar, I was the only one with a flat stomach who could bench press more than his weight.

The bell rang promptly at seven twenty and everyone moved to the tables, some more eagerly than others, the women taking seats against the wall as was the custom, and the men forming an inner-circle facing them. The evening's host, an attractive gal whom I would've liked hooking up with, reminded everyone of the rules: five minutes per date; no lingering; gents move to the next table to their left, women remain seated. "Be sure to use the date pamphlet," she reminded us, which would be collected afterward and used by the organizers to link us up later. She stressed that dating concluded promptly at nine, but anyone wishing to remain afterward was welcome to do so. It pretty much followed the same format as the others I'd attended. And then it was post time.

My first date, Shelly, a petite thing from Pittsburgh with nervous eyes, had a shy voice that was quickly lost in the rising tide of conversations around us, forcing me to lean over the votive candle in the center of the table to better hear her. She offered a timid hand which I must have held too long, judging from the way she withdrew it. I asked about her work and she used our remaining time grousing about her job as a researcher at the Patent and Trade Office and the lack of available men there. I did my best to appear interested and was glad when the five-minute bell rang.

Date number two, the antithesis of my first date, was fit and trim, wore her blonde hair short and had penetrating eyes that locked onto mine with an air of confidence that shook my world. Rather than offer her hand, she kept them crossed in front of her at the wrist. After introductions, she admitted to being thirty-six, twice divorced and sans children. When I admired the dragon tattoo climbing her sculptured bicep, she raised her sleeve, revealing its extended crimson tongue, saying, "My zodiac sign. I was born in the year of the dragon. Ancient Chinese believe the dragon's the ultimate symbol of cosmic chi. Chi means energy," she explained.

"I know," I said. "I'm a student of feng shui."

Nodding her approval, she said, "Then you know the dragon is the most potent symbol in the Chinese pantheon. It represents good fortune."

I didn't, and shook my head.

"What's your sign?" she asked.

"Sagittarius. The archer."

She frowned. "What *year* were you born?"

I was tempted to shave off a few but sensed she'd know I was lying. "March sixty-three," I said, eliciting another frown.

"The fertile, vulnerable rabbit feels the tremors and call of springtime more than most creatures, and responds in wild courtship," she said.

"I never thought of it that way," I said, recalling how fast and hard I had fallen for Carol Rutter, the naval officer I encountered during a previous case, which, I noted, occurred during springtime. Intrigued, I said, "Please go on."

"The rabbit also tends to be trustworthy, empathetic, and a willing caregiver," she informed me.

I was fascinated. I've been looking after my estranged spinster sister in the nursing home for several years, though not very *willingly*. The task had fallen to me, her only relative, after her stroke. As for trustworthy and empathetic, well, I thought, aren't most folks? "Anything else?" I said, enjoying our time together.

"We're not compatible, you and I," she said to my disappointment.

"I might disagree," I said. "You don't know me."

"Doesn't matter," she countered.

"It does to me."

"You're persistent. I like that."

"Anything worth having is worth fighting for," I said.

She clicked her tongue. "Perhaps. But you'd do well to pair up with someone born in the year of the sheep or the boar."

"What if I'm attracted to the dragon?"

She shook her head. "I'm too energetic for you. You can't keep up with me."

I grinned. "Let's give it a try."

She smiled knowingly just as the bell rang. "Good luck."

Despite the brush-off, I scribbled her name tag number on my date sheet, hoping she'd do the same after meeting the others.

The next several dates, while pleasant enough, were unremarkable, possibly because my thoughts were still with the dragon lady. Occasionally, I'd glance in her direction, hoping to catch her eye, but her attention was always on the person seated across from her, as it had been with me. Once, I saw her leaning forward and smiling with more enthusiasm than she'd shown me or the others, and I figured this one must be a zodiac soul mate—someone born in the year of the rat or the monkey, as she'd said. Probably the rat, I thought, noting his angular features and retro rattail braid hanging below his shoulders.

"Hi, I'm Pam Biddle," my next date said, offering a warm smile and firm handshake. Then, eyeing my name tag, "Is that a misspelling?"

"No, it's correct. The full name's Jerzy Shore."

"Seriously?"

"'Fraid so." I was used to these exchanges, having experienced them throughout my adult life—I won't mention my childhood other than to say I learned how to defend myself at an early age. "Two alcoholic parents with a warped sense of humor," I explained.

"I guess you're going to tell me you're from Atlantic City, or someplace like that," she said.

"Actually, Bayonne. Know what they call people from Bayonne?" She shook her head, and I said, "Bayonets."

Her expression didn't change—not even a smile—and I thought, I must be losing my touch.

"Must've been tough growing up," she said.

"You have no idea."

"Oh, yes I do. I'm from Riddle, Oregon, and we lived on Whittle Drive."

"Well, Miss Biddle from Riddle, it's a pleasure meeting you."

That brought a smile and we quickly fell into swapping anecdotes, then groaned when the bell rang. "We should do this over lunch," I suggested.

"Yes we should," she agreed, but I noticed she didn't write my tag number on her date sheet.

It was ten of nine, and I had two more tables to visit.

Sad to say, my next-to-last date had one too many mai tais by the time I reached her—three empty glasses and one near-empty one cluttered the table. Regrettably, she was not a happy drunk, and I sat there listening to her whine about her ex-boyfriend, who, as it turned out, was a fellow NCIS agent from Norfolk, who, she informed me between frequent sips, was a fucking liar who had no intention of divorcing his—sip—wife.

"The cad," I said.

I knew him professionally. We had worked several cases together, but I wasn't about to tell her, or that he had never been married. He'd played her, and I wondered how often he used that line. I hadn't thought highly of him before tonight—he was a middling agent who showed little initiative in solving our shared cases—and now I thought even less of him.

"What do you do?" she finally asked as the clock wound down.

I could see me wearing what remained of her mai tai if I told her. Instead, I said, "I'm a private investigator," and watched her grimace.

"Shit! Just my luck."

"We aren't all alike," I said.

She snorted. "I'll bet."

"No, really," I protested, but she'd already tuned me out.

As I moved to the next table I overheard her snap at the poor soul taking my seat, "You better not be a goddamn cop."

My final date introduced herself with the enthusiasm of a wet dishrag. "Long day?" I asked.

"Been coming to these things nearly a year. Don't know why."

She was plain looking, a tad on the frumpy side, and of an indeterminate age. Still, with a little effort she could be attractive.

"And it hasn't worked out?" I asked.

"I'll let you in on a secret. Never tell someone you're a lawyer."

"Why not?"

She shook her head. "Nobody likes lawyers. So now, I say I'm a flight attendant."

"And that works?"

"It keeps the conversation going."

"What kind of law do you practice?"

She winked. "I'm a stewardess."

I wasn't interested in playing that game, and asked, "Have you tried different speed dating groups?"

"Tried 'em all," she said with a sour laugh. "Gen Ys, Gen Xs, Baby Boomers, Professionals, Asian, Muslim, Jewish, Christian. Even a bisexual session."

"How'd that go? The bisexual one?"

She shrugged. "Not bad, actually."

I wasn't enjoying her failures, but I was curious. "How about dating websites?" I'd considered trying one, but hadn't yet.

"Been there. Match.com, Meetyourspouse.com, Cupidsmates.com. Lotta weirdoes out there."

I listened, wondering if this is what I had to look forward to, a string of disappointments.

In the next instant she laid her hand on mine. "What are you doing afterward? Gonna hang around?" she asked.

I shook my head. "Heading home."

"Where's that?"

"Over the bridge, in Virginia."

"How about a lift? I'm in Arlington," she said.

This was not how I wanted to end my evening, bedding a desperate woman. "Can't," I said.

When the final bell rang she tightened her grip and

offered a tired smile. "You sure? Might be fun."

I had no interest in being the duty stud and, with as much compassion as I could muster, I said, "Perhaps another time," and watched her hand slip away.

I stood and looked around. The dragon lady was across the room, heading for the door. Damn, I thought, I would've liked another shot at her. Before leaving, she turned and smiled at me. At least, I think it was meant for me. Then she was gone.

THREE

Laura bolted awake soaked in perspiration and in the usual agitated state. This time, pushing herself up, she trudged downstairs and headed to her computer rather than her cigarettes. What, she wondered staring at the blank screen, would she write to Leo Kleinman this time? With her fingers resting on the keyboard, she shifted her gaze to the scorched piece of *Liberty* handrail in the bookcase across the room, one of the souvenirs salvaged from the ship prior to it being scrapped, and shuddered.

Dear Leo…,

She began using his first name because she felt closer to him after moving to Butner, not because he responded to her letters; he couldn't. They were sent anonymously. Moreover, she wasn't interested in anything he might say. She had read enough about the jailed traitor to know how he would respond, if he could.

Like every prisoner's mail, Kleinman's was opened, read and checked for contraband, and so she could reasonably expect that what she wrote would filter through the system. Knowing traitors were among the most despised inmates in the prison population, she embarked on her writing campaign hoping her letters might induce an inmate to attack him for rejecting his country and swearing allegiance to a country that killed thirty-four Americans and injured one hundred and seventy-one of their shipmates in an unprovoked attack on the *Liberty*.

In previous letters she disputed Israel's claims, saying it was ludicrous to think the sophisticated Israeli Defense Force might confuse an Egyptian horse carrier with an American naval vessel more than twice its size and fitted with an elaborate array of antennas. She also cited sources disputing Israel's claim the ship had fired its guns at troops ashore, noting *Liberty* was thirteen miles off shore when attacked, far beyond the two-mile effective range of her 50-caliber machine guns.

Now, sitting at her computer in her bed clothes, Laura turned away from the damaged handrail and began writing.

How's the traitor today??!! No doubt you knew from the envelope this would be from me! Who else sends anonymous letters??? I bet I'm the only one! How's it feel having these letters read by the mail room staff?? Does it make you nervous knowing your allegiance to Israel might incite a patriot to end your life? Frankly, I'm surprised you survived this long surrounded by Americans who don't cotton to traitors and don't buy your BS about being a political prisoner. Wouldn't they be surprised to know the Israelis deposit $10,000 in your bank account every month. Some say $5,000, but I heard $10,000. Whatever, all that tax-free money is there waiting for you when you get out. A nice nest egg (over $3,500,000) for selling out your country!!!

I wonder what your fellow inmates think about that!!

Laura pushed away from her desk, rolling her shoulders. She considered having a cigarette but returned to the letter instead.

While death is what you deserve, I'd be content if someone gave you a severe beating that left you with injuries like Liberty crewmen endured. Injuries that cause mind-bending visions that interrupt your sleep, or blur your eyesight, leaving you disoriented and with debilitating headaches so your forced to rely on strangers to feed and dress and wash you. A brain-rattling blow to your head would do it! Just like your new country did to our sailors!!

Laura watched her letter emerge from the printer while leaning back and rubbing her neck. She was so tired. Had there been time she would have included some of the gory details of the attack—details she'd heard from her uncle and his shipmates at *Liberty* reunions—that now colored her dreams, but there wasn't time. The sky was turning gray, and she was due at the prison in three hours.

FOUR

Theo, our forensics expert and part-time, semi-professional food eating contestant, looked up as I passed his cluttered office. "Hey, Iceman," he called with a grin. "How goes the speed dating?"

The Iceman nickname evolved from a personalized license plate I kept along with other law enforcement memorabilia in my office. It was presented to me by the Norfolk PD for helping close a troublesome cold case involving a sailor and a dead hooker. Taking the joke a step further, my fellow NCIS agents gave me a set of business cards inscribed with *Iceman*.

"Erratic," I replied.

"Erotic?" Theo said with a wider grin. "Sounds interesting."

"ERRATIC!" I repeated, and then told him about the alluring Dragon Lady. "I wrote her info on the turn-in sheet," I said with a shrug, "but haven't heard anything yet."

"She sounds erotic to me," Theo said. Then, shifting his gaze to my hair, he said, "*That* puts you in the game."

The hair transplant, now six months old, had gone well, I thought. The new crop blending perfectly with the old, covering my receding hairline. It was eleven thousand dollars well spent.

My hand automatically went to it. "You think so?" I said, patting the new growth.

"Yep. That, and the dye job take ten years off."

Unlike the ragging I'd gotten from the other agents, I knew Theo was sincere. He might be too candid at times, but he wasn't a wise-ass. "It'll look even fuller in a few months, they tell me."

"No doubt. Maybe I'll get one someday," he said.

I had decided on the transplant after my last failed attempt at romance—that and trimming my waistline. The waist was easy, more gym time and less fried food. The hair problem required research. A few agents suggested Rogaine, saying it worked for them. But I didn't want something that worked only for long as I used it. And since I wasn't interested in a toupee, that left two options; hair weaving or the pricier transplant.

"Where you heading?" Theo asked.

"To see the chief," I said of John Scully, the assistant director for Criminal Investigations. "One of those, drop-everything-and-come-see-me, summons."

Theo shook his head. "Funny. For a cold case maven, you draw a lotta short fuse ones."

"Not so funny," I said.

"I didn't mean ha ha funny."

"I know." Good ol' Theo. I was indebted to him for saving my life a while back, when a vengeful ex-sailor I'd arrested and helped prosecute tried burning down my house with me in it after being released. Had it not been for Theo's quick thinking the perp might have succeeded.

"Reporting for duty as ordered, Mein Führer," I said, clicking my heels before *Miss Disagreeable's* desk. I had long ago ceased acknowledging Scully's gatekeeper by name because of her abrasive manner toward those of lesser rank than her boss, which naturally included me.

Without interrupting her gum chewing, or looking up from her computer, she said, "You may go in."

As I passed her desk I considered swiping one of her cherished Beanie Babies—probably the only collection still around—but doing so would only cause Scully heartburn, which he didn't need.

I knocked and braced myself for the flow of bad chi awaiting me inside. My frequent suggestions to use a few simple feng shui techniques to reduce, if not eliminate, the negative energy swirling around his office were routinely rebuffed, rather rudely I thought. So, in keeping with our truce, I no longer raise the issue and Scully no longer throws me out of his office.

"What's up, Chief?" I asked.

"Sit." His heavy tone suggested this wasn't a social call, not that my visits ever were. "We got a hot one," he said, pushing a file in my direction.

I've since learned whenever Scully begins our meetings with *we*, it's *me* who winds up with the problem. Seeing LEO KLEINMAN stamped on the cover, I picked it up and asked, "This the traitor?"

He replied with a tired nod. "The same."

Kleinman had worked for naval intelligence as a civilian analyst with the Anti-Terrorist Alert Center, which gave him unfettered access to highly classified documents that he shopped around at various embassies until making a deal with the Israelis in exchange for cash and ultimately Israeli citizenship. Regrettably, before the thefts were discovered much of the information—our attack plans against the Soviets and analyses of their missile systems, much of it gleaned from Soviet sources who were later executed once their identities became known—had been bartered in exchange for Soviet Jewish émigrés. This all transpired back in the mid-eighties, which, I figured, was probably why Scully considered it a cold case, and was about to drop it in my lap.

I opened the folder and skimmed the top page, noting, "He's still at Butner. Which means he's the Bureau of Prisons' problem, not ours."

He sighed. "Nothing's ever that simple. Since his incarceration, Israel has petitioned every president to commute his sentence. Now, with Snowden's disclosures the Israelis know we've been spying on them."

"So?"

"So they've decided to take a new approach to Kleinman. The prime minister's claiming we're adhering to a double standard keeping him imprisoned. Says that isn't how trusted allies behave."

"Trusted allies! Aren't we still waiting for our *trusted allies* to return the shitload of documents that SOB passed to them?" I said, and watched Sully wince.

"True," he said.

Prompting me to add, "And what about those Israeli agents, the ones recruiting over here?" I was making no attempt to disguise my anger. "How's that fit in with their concept of trusted allies?"

"They aren't the only friendlies spying on us," he reminded me.

That was true. I also knew I wasn't going to win this argument. Taking a long breath, I asked, "So, how do *we* fit into this?"

If he noticed my little taunt, he ignored it. "It's fallen to us to keep the bastard alive," he said.

Oops. Scully, a practicing Christian, rarely used foul language and rarely tolerated it from us. So he had to be feeling pressure from above, which cued me to tone down my rhetoric.

"You lost me, Chief. He's in federal prison where he

belongs. What's NCIS got to do with keeping him alive? And why would we want to?"

"Like I said, it's complicated. The Palestinians are signaling they're ready to move forward with a peace accord, but the Israelis are dragging their feet. To get them to the table, one of the carrots we're offering is the possibility of Kleinman's release."

"What?"

"Kleinman's a hero over there."

"No doubt. And he'll be a bigger hero when he reveals what's locked up in that photographic memory of his. Casper Weinberger was right. We should've shot the bastard."

"That didn't happen," Scully said, "and now he's a State Department asset, a pawn in the peace process."

I couldn't help myself, and I said, "Whoever came up with this idea, Chief, has their head you-know-where if they believe releasing Kleinman'll bring those two factions together. Tells you what a sham this peace business is."

The negative energy was tearing into the back of my neck and sending a sharp pain to my hip, causing me to shift my chair to the side.

Scully raised an eyebrow. "You aren't going to start in with that Kung Fu hocus pocus again?"

"It's *feng shui*, Chief. And no, I'm not going to tell you what a bad situation you have here and how easy it is to fix by rearranging your furniture and bringing in a few plants and crystals."

"There you go, you just did."

"Did what?"

"Told me."

"Sorry."

"Now that we got that out of the way, can we get back to keeping Kleinman alive?" Scully said, his voice growing weary.

I twisted my neck and heard a loud crack. "Is that why I'm here?" And when he nodded, I said, "I can't wait."

FIVE

Leo Kleinman was grateful for the break in routine, where every day had the same dull rhythm. Snapping open his combination lock, he retrieved a clean set of khakis from his locker, which were washed and pressed weekly by another inmate at the going rate of one book of postage stamps per month, stamps being the underground currency at Butner, where prisoners are prohibited from possessing or handling money. Until 2004, when tobacco products were banned, the underground currency throughout the federal prison system had been cigarettes. Now the currency varied from prison to prison, as he had learned from inmates transferring in from other facilities. Whereas it was stamps at Butner, at other places it might be something as obscure as packets of dried tuna or mackerel (macks, as they were called), or other commonly stocked items in the commissary system that were easily transferable when paying debts, securing black market items, or services, such as laundry, haircuts or protection.

Today was Tuesday, and the clean uniform was for Ruth's benefit when she arrived at two thirty for her twice-monthly visit. They had determined early on that scheduling visits mid-week worked best. Hotels near the prison were cheaper then and traffic along the I-95/I-85 corridor was lighter. Plus, weekday visits counted for one visitor point against the allotted sixteen per month, while weekend visits counted for four points, thereby allowing Kleinman points to accommodate delegates from the Israeli embassy or others from his network of supporters. As an added bonus, the Visitors Room tended to be less crowded on weekdays, thus providing a tad more privacy with his beloved Ruth.

As he dressed, his gaze fell to the rear of his locker and the anonymous rambling letters from his tormentor. And while it troubled him that they grew more vitriolic, it bothered him more that the writer was fixated upon linking the unfortunate USS *Liberty* incident to his personal mission of aiding Israel. By his reckoning, the one clearly had nothing to do with the other. Over the years, he had received probably hundreds of angry letters from Americans, many graphically threatening great bodily harm given the opportunity, but rarely had anyone continued writing after venting his anger, as this one was doing. Clearly, this writer's motivation went beyond anger. As Kleinman saw it, connecting him to the *Liberty* attack made no sense; he was twelve at the time, and barely aware of the episode. Still, he would like to meet this person, to present Israel's side of the attack now that he had educated himself about the facts, but that didn't seem likely, he thought, buttoning his shirt.

Kleinman closed his locker, adjusted his yarmulke, smoothed his beard, and headed across the drab, gray campus for the admin building, where he'd wait to be called out once Ruth had completed checking in.

The Federal Correctional Institution at Butner consisted of four separate units; Low, Medium-I, Medium-II, and the Medical Center. Kleinman was in

Medium-I's Clemson Unit—where the dormitory-style units drew their names from Atlantic Coast Conference colleges. Segregated from the rest of the prison, Medium-I, with its exercise facilities, was known among inmates, their family and friends, and members of the news media as Camp Fluffy.

Passing Georgia Tech and the adjoining volleyball court, Kleinman glanced at his watch and quickened his pace. It was two twenty-eight, Sarah would be in the admin building now, and he was tempted to break the rules and run, but thought better of it.

Unlike most inmates, he maintained a clean disciplinary record and wished to keep it that way. Too many incident reports—known as *shots*—would curtail prized privileges, some granted because of his religious preference, such as kosher meals and numerous Jewish holy days, when he was excused from work. Only the American Indians had more holidays, which riled him as much as their sweat lodge did, where they gathered weekly out from under the constant view of the guards. It was a sweet deal, he thought, before reminding himself any inmate could change his religion at any time, and many did to gain additional privileges. Religion in prison was flexible. At one point, he had even declared himself an American Indian, before returning to Judaism.

Meanwhile, Ruth was at the main entrance, affirming on BOP Form A224.022 for the umpteenth time that she did not have on her person firearms, explosives, weapons, ammunition, metal cutting tools, recording equipment, cellular phone, narcotics, marijuana, camera, food items, alcohol, or prescription drugs. On signing the form, she further stated she understood she could not leave the visiting area and return; that once she walked out the visit was terminated.

With the completed form in hand, she entered the office and submitted it and her Maryland driver's license to the duty officer where, under the hungry stares of trustees, she waited for him to verify she was on the list of approved visitors. Next, she handed over her purse for inspection, feeling the weight of twenty dollars in quarters for use in the prison vending machines. That done, she crossed the hall to the Visitors Room and joined those waiting for their inmates to be summoned.

Moments later, she and Kleinman were embracing and holding a long kiss, the only physical contact authorized until she departed.

"What would you like?" she asked as they settled into their assigned seats.

Any attempt at privacy was lost as others arrived. Occasionally, a guard strolled through, but the preferred method of monitoring inmates and visitors was through snitches. Everyone knew the rats and despised them, especially the ones coming through under the pretext of dispensing candy to the children.

"Nachos, Coke and two cheese sandwiches to begin with," he replied. It no longer annoyed him that he was prohibited from touching so much as a lousy quarter for the vending machines, or that they were prohibited from sharing whatever snacks she purchased. The rules were clear. Nothing was to be exchanged between them, especially not the two crisp twenty-dollar bills folded and pressed into a single tiny square and hidden in her waistband, which she'd pass to him at an appropriate time later. Unlike some cons' wives and girlfriends—especially the younger, uninitiated ones, who looked as nervous as cats when making their first switch—Ruth could make these exchanges without the slightest tell.

Kleinman often mused how they would have made a great pair of thieves on the outside. She had it all, beauty, a disarming personality and, most importantly, chutzpah. Buoyed by the inmate code—you rate what you get away with—he'd encouraged her to pass along all sorts of contraband, which she did without breaking a sweat. Once, at his request, she'd even slipped him her soiled panties to fantasize over.

"You're eating all the wrong foods," she said, returning from the vending machines.

He shrugged reaching for them. There were few pleasures in prison, and he routinely disregarded guidelines encouraging a healthy lifestyle, eating what he pleased while limiting his exercise to occasional games of bocce, horseshoes or slow walks around the exercise track. When he wasn't earning $3.34 a week cutting cloth for U.S. Army utility shirts, a cushy job acquired after two years on the waiting list, he spent much of his free time reading. Consequently, he was now forty pounds overweight.

Kleinman had watched Ruth walk to the vending machines, taking pleasure in knowing other inmates were enjoying the view as much as he. His gaze followed her long, sculpted legs, made shapelier by high heels, and lingered on her tight ass. His breathing grew shallow as he reached down and touched himself. She was stunning; as stunning as the day they first met, when she arrived at the prison in that tight-fitting pink knit Chanel suit heading a delegation of B'nai B'rith supporters seeking his release. Seeing her then, he knew he had to marry her.

She was a marvelous woman. Who else would make the four hundred-mile round trip, oversee his website, manage his fan mail, and court the media without complaining?

"What's bothering you, Leo?" she asked, as he tore open his first sandwich.

He took a large bite, chewed and swallowed. "Bread is stale."

"I didn't mean the sandwich."

Knowing she wasn't going to let it go, he said, "It's that damn letter writer. He won't quit."

"What is it now?"

He waved the half-eaten sandwich, unconcerned with the crumbs falling in his lap, and said, "More of the same gibberish, blaming our homeland for the *Liberty* attack. And spelling out how those crewmen suffered."

"If only we could help him understand," she said, while he stuffed his mouth.

"What's to understand? He doesn't once mention Hamas, or Hezbollah or the Holocaust. All he talks about is that *farshlepteh* spy ship." He shook his head. "Won't acknowledge the death camps. Or how the survivors built a state, revived a language, and created a land of hope when no one stepped forward to help. Instead, he criticizes."

"There's something else bothering you. You can tell me." She reached out to stroke his face and lowered her hand when a trustee entered the room.

Kleinman was into his bag of Nachos now, the orange powder and crumbs tinting his gray beard. "You can't take what these screwballs say to heart," he said. "It's their way of venting," he said, trying to put her off.

"But this one's been venting for some time," she countered.

"We've heard such rantings before. It's nothing," he insisted.

Leaning in close, she whispered, "This one is different, isn't he? Tell me. Maybe I can help."

"You're a saint," he said, snatching the folded bills she'd transferred into her palm and slipping them inside his sock. "The shmuck wants me dead."

"He isn't the first one," she said. "I recall Secretary of Defense Weinberger wanted you executed. What else?" she pressed.

Kleinman adjusted his wire-rimmed glasses. "He's trying to create hostility."

"How?"

"Using his letters to reach the others. Hoping to incite someone to come after me."

"But inmates don't open your mail, the staff does."

"Bubbala, I live in a closed society. Word spreads like wildfire in here. People talk. If he plants an idea… Gets some sympathetic Jew-hater riled up, well… You see what could happen?"

"You have friends," she said. "Surely they'll protect you."

"I thought you understood. Friendship in prison is meaningless. It exists only as long as it benefits someone. The instant that equation changes, friendship dissolves. There are no exceptions."

Ruth wouldn't be put off. "Have you talked with your case manager or counselor?"

He snorted, sending Nacho crumbs flying. "They don't have time for vague or perceived threats."

"There must be a way of stopping this madness."

"I'll let you know when I think of one." He looked at his watch and stood. "It's almost four."

She waited while he joined the others in the hall for the four o'clock head count. When he returned they talked about her dealings with support groups, and of new friends acquired through the website *Justice for Leo Kleinman*.

"I met a nice Persian Jew at synagogue," she told him. "He lives near us." She was always careful to let him know she considered her apartment in Bethesda, Maryland, theirs. That he had a place to come home to when he was finally released. "He's a man of means. He owns a successful Oriental rug business. He wants to help."

Kleinman smiled. "Good. See if you can get him to see the president."

It was nearing dinnertime when she returned to the rest room, inserting a paper towel where the lock had been, indicating the room was occupied. There, she removed a cocaine-filled capsule from her bra and popped it into her mouth, then flushed before exiting.

When she emerged, they walked to the door together, where they embraced and kissed, she pressing the capsule into his mouth with her tongue.

"I love you," she said afterward and watched him leave.

SIX

I exited Scully's office with Kleinman's file tucked firmly beneath my arm and headed downstairs, the crick in my neck disappearing soon afterward. My first chore would be contacting the Federal Bureau of Prisons to learn what I could about prisoner 298746-724, but not before checking in with Theo.

When I arrived at his office, his nose was buried in a monograph detailing what motivates killers to alter death scenes by repositioning victims' bodies. There seemed to be no aspect of forensic science that didn't intrigue him. Leroy, his life-size bloodstained mannequin, which he used to demonstrate spatter patterns to agents, hung from its pedestal behind him, its bloodied head tilted down as if gazing over Theo's shoulder. It was a bizarre scene to the uninitiated.

"What do you know about anonymous threatening letters?" I asked.

Theo looked up and grinned. "One of your former girlfriends?"

"Not a chance. When they walk out, it's for good," I said. "This is business."

His grin changed to a frown. "Not another mysterious midshipman death?" he asked, recalling a previous cold case that began with an anonymous letter and ended with me entangled with the Navy's top brass.

I shook my head. "This one's wackier." I gave him a quick rundown on Kleinman and the letters he claimed to have received.

Theo responded as I had to Scully minutes earlier. "Why are you getting involved? Seems like a job for the FBI."

"Exactly what I told the chief."

He raised his hand. "Lemme guess. FBI said it belongs in our wheelhouse."

"Right," I said. "By their reckoning, it's ours because we made the case against Kleinman."

"Because they were too busy to get involved," Theo noted. "And now they're too busy again. And since we're a federal agency, they're happy to turn it over to us."

"Right on all counts."

"That is until it's time to get the glory," he added. "Like they did when Kleinman made a run for the Israeli embassy and they stepped in for the arrest. It's déjà vu all over again."

"So, what can you tell me about analyzing anonymous letters?"

Theo went to one of his crammed bookcases. "Not a whole lot," he said crouching and scanning a row of titles. "It's an evolving field. Mostly academicians, with much of their funding coming from Homeland Security these days. Here!" he said, coming up with a professional journal and flipping it open. "Read this article on psycholinguistics. It's drawn from a paper delivered by a doctoral candidate to a joint anti-terrorist seminar in Quantico last year. Take it with you. And don't overlook the endnotes. You might find someone listed there who can help you."

Good, old Theo. He never disappoints. I don't know

his IQ, but I'd bet it's in the stratosphere. I thanked him and left. My next task was to find the right person in the Bureau of Prisons. I made a few calls and lined up a meeting for the following day.

*　*　*

The BOP, located in the former Federal Home Loan Bank Board Building, wasn't far from our satellite office at the Washington Navy Yard. I showed my ID and was directed to a conference room on the third floor, where I found David Cullen, the assistant to the director of the Mid-Atlantic region. He was seated at a table in an otherwise empty room, his hands clasped atop a thick folder and a not-too-pleasant air about him.

He remained seated when I entered. His manner suggesting he had far more important issues on his plate than driving in from his Annapolis office to accommodate me. Considering the twenty federal prisons in his region, I made it a point to thank him for seeing me on short notice.

He nodded and motioned me to a chair across from him. "So, Leo Kleinman's become important again," he said.

I nodded. "Who would've thought after all these years."

"And now you're going to babysit the little prick."

"Not quite. I'm here to figure out who's out there stirring up the pot, so I can put an end to his shenanigans. As I see it, keeping Kleinman alive is still your responsibility."

"Well," he said, his facial muscles tightening, "we've been doing all right up to now."

Oops. Institutional battle lines were being drawn with Cullen asserting BOP had everything under control, and my presence suggesting otherwise. It was time to step back. "I'm not here to get into your knickers. I don't know enough about your end of the business to even attempt it. Like I said, my goal is to ID the guy sending the letters. To be honest, I don't give a rat's ass what happens to the traitor. But, unfortunately, my opinion doesn't count much around here."

He nodded. "At least we agree he's a piece of shit. So how can we help?"

"I need to learn as much as possible about Kleinman. What type of prisoner he is, what his routine is, who he pals around with, who visits him, who he communicates with. Anything that'll give me a lead."

Cullen opened his folder and withdrew a sheet of paper. "Let's start with the man. This psychological profile was put together at our medical center in Springfield, Missouri, shortly after sentencing. Portions of it probably confirm what you folks already know, like his photographic memory."

"From what I understand, his memory's remarkable. I read that at his pre-sentencing agreement he identified over eight hundred classified publications and a thousand secret and top secret messages and cables he sold to the Israelis. I'm lucky to remember yesterday's lunch."

Cullen didn't respond. Instead, his eyes went to the paper and he read, "Despite possessing an inflated sense of self-importance and a keen desire for recognition, subject lives in a fantasy world, often confusing fantasy with reality. He is highly intelligent, as reflected by his 187 IQ. He is an expert at manipulation and deceit." Pausing, Cullen looked up, and said, "In other words, he's a con man. So when you sit down with him, be careful." Reading on, he said, "Subject shows no remorse for his crimes. Instead, he takes great pride in them. Subtlety is not one of subject's strong points."

"That's about it," he said, replacing the paper.

"What kind of prisoner is he?"

"First, I'll outline the protocol," he said, leaning back and steepling his fingers. "Every inmate's progress is monitored by his unit team." His voice, like his expression, remained flat, without change or pitch, as if delivering a rote lecture to a class of raw recruits. "Each team is located in or directly adjacent to an inmate housing unit, ensuring close supervision. The team consists of a unit manager, case manager, correctional counselor and unit officer. And while it's made clear to each inmate that they develop and maintain a positive relationship with members of their unit team, it's also stressed that does not mean they should come running to them with every problem.

"As you can imagine, these folks have large caseloads, and they encourage inmates to work out their problems before coming to them. Kleinman understands this and adheres to the guidelines. As determined by the unit team, he obeys the rules. Though, with his brains he's probably scamming the system. He started out in Petersburg, Virginia, then went to Springfield, Missouri, for his physical and psychological evaluation, then to Marion, Illinois, where he spent five years in isolation — spies aren't popular among the inmate population — before transferring to Butner in 1993."

"Where he's been a model prisoner?" I said.

Cullen laughed. "Hardly. Soon after arriving, the weasel passed classified info to the *Jerusalem Post* in an interview. That won't happen again. Now, all sanctioned interviews are monitored by a rep from Office of Naval Intelligence or National Security Agency."

"What about routine correspondence?" I asked.

"All inmate mail is opened and checked for

contraband. No exceptions. In Kleinman's case we read every incoming and outgoing letter."

"The same with his emails?"

"You familiar with TRULINCS?"

"The inmate email system," I said. "I've heard of it."

He nodded. "All incoming and outgoing emails are also checked. It's a limited system. Inmates can only communicate with pre-approved contacts. And it doesn't permit attachments, photos, graphics, or the like. There are other restrictions, as well. The program doesn't allow access to the Internet. And inmates who solicited minors for sexual activity, or are charged with possession of or distribution of child pornography, are excluded from it."

"What about mail from his attorneys?" I asked.

"The rules apply to everyone. The envelope has to be marked *Special Mail-Open in the Presence of the Inmate*. Correspondence must be on attorney letterhead, bearing the attorney's name. Still, we check it for contraband like all other correspondence, but we don't read it." He saw me frown and reminded me, "Attorneys are officers of the court. They'd have to be really stupid to screw up."

When I said, "I've known quite a few stupid ones," he let the comment slide, making me think he might hold a law degree. Oh, well.

When I asked, "Who's on his visitor list?" he produced another page.

"The immediate family that was verified in his presentence report and subsequently amended. That would be Kleinman's wife, his parents and his brother, plus a couple of delegates from the Israeli embassy, and his attorneys. Those are the permanent ones. Others may be added on an ad hoc basis."

"His wife? I thought she divorced him."

"This is number two. They were married after number

one was released from prison. When she returned to Canada, she divorced him."

"Who would marry this turd?"

"You haven't visited his website, have you?"

"I didn't know he had one."

"Check it out. He's got quite a following. You'd think he was the Dalai Lama. This one married him after he arrived at Butner."

"Can I get a copy of the visitor list?"

Cullen nodded.

"Who's he pal around with?"

"Inmates don't trust each other, so they're constantly shifting allegiances, except for ethnic and gay cliques, who pretty much stay together," he said, flipping a page. "Says here, he tends to be a loner. Outside of work, he can be found with fellow lifers when he isn't in his cubicle reading. He's not into sports or other activities. Prefers the library and occasionally uses the exercise track during recreation periods. He eats with Jews in the mess hall. There's a note says he entertains new arrivals with ghoulish tales of prison life."

"Entertains them, or frightens them?"

"As I'm sure you know, life inside doesn't bring out the best in men," Cullen replied. "They may call Kleinman's section Camp Fluffy, but just because they aren't splitting rocks doesn't mean it's a picnic. They're told where to be, when to be there, when to eat and when to sleep. During the work-day, every inmate must have a pass to move from one area to another. Every day is essentially the same, and boredom is a constant problem. There are five headcounts scheduled around the clock, plus frequent unannounced lockdowns. They have no privacy, and they're always vigilant, lest they offend or insult some nutcake."

No sympathy here, I thought. They broke the law,

and deserve what they get.

"How do you assess the threat posed by the letters?" I asked.

He shrugged. "He's been inside nearly thirty years. Nobody pays him much attention anymore. He's just another old-timer now. Still, there's the possibility the letters might incite someone, especially with what's going on around the world."

"Then why don't you just put him back in solitary?"

"We can't just put him in the SHU because of those letters."

"Shoe? What's a shoe?"

"That's what we call solitary now. The special housing unit."

"Seems like a good place for him."

"He didn't think so when he was there. Not many men do. Twenty-three hours in lock-up isn't appealing, no matter how safe it is. You spend enough time alone, without privileges and without the little freedom you do have, and you'll take your chances in the general population. Kleinman's no fool. Given the choice, he'll stay out of the SHU and let us carry the load."

"Even with the letters coming in?"

"Of course he's concerned. We all are. Still, until something happens, or we learn something may happen, he'll continue relying on us to maintain order." When I fell quiet, he gazed at his watch, and asked, "Anything else?"

"When can I get a copy of the letters?"

"You could if we had them." Noting my surprise, he said, "We have no reason to keep 'em. They're his property."

"So I'll have to go down to Butner and get them from him?"

"I think I can save you a trip. Ask over at the Israeli

Embassy. I'm sure they'd be happy to help you."

"The Israelis?"

Cullen laughed. "Kleinman trusts them more than he trusts us."

"What a whacky world we live in."

"How long you been doing this?" Cullen asked.

I thought about that, and said, "You're right. I keep forgetting. This is Washington, where nothing makes sense. Most of my cases are outside the Beltway, where life is much simpler, not like this screwy town."

"Screwy? I'da said, fucked up."

I heaved a sigh. Considering their role in Kleinman's thefts, I didn't expect much from the Israelis. Still, with few leads, what choice did I have? "What about that visitor list?"

"You'll have it tomorrow."

I left Cullen thinking Scully had done it to me again, dropped me somewhere in the middle of Bazarro World.

SEVEN

Unlike her fitful nights, Laura's days as a dental hygienist at the prison were routine, up at six, shower, dress and out the door by six thirty. At that hour, her pattern varied little from the other bleary-eyed regulars at the McDonald's on Highway 56, where a nod or quick smile sufficed as a greeting, which suited her fine, particularly after a fitful night's sleep. At such times, seeking to be alone, she'd take her Dollar Breakfast Menu meal and newspaper to a distant table away from the other diners. By seven thirty, she'd head to the prison, her mind focused on the tasks ahead. But not so today.

Laura had barely swallowed her first bite when the headline *U.S. Considers Release for Israeli Spy Kleinman* leapt off the page at her. She blinked hard, certain she'd misread it. But she hadn't. Impossible, she thought, catching her breath. She knew enough about his case to know he didn't deserve to be freed. But now the president was declaring he was prepared to do just that as a means of shoring up the faltering U.S.-brokered Middle East peace talks. Her hand trembling, Laura pushed away her uneaten breakfast.

Linking Kleinman to the peace talks was preposterous. It made no sense. How could his release possibly add to discussions half a world away? Surely, the Israelis and Palestinians were focused on far more important issues than Leo Kleinman. Yet, according to an unnamed government source, he was indeed a player. His release from prison would boost the Israeli prime minister's standing at a time when his coalition government was close to breaking up, thereby enabling him to grant concessions deemed important to the Palestinians.

"This is bullshit!" she blurted, turning nearby heads.

Reading on, she learned no decision had been made yet, but should the president decide to release him, he could do so immediately by commuting Kleinman's sentence or waiting and releasing him the following year, when the spy became eligible for parole. Reading on, she grimaced at the stale arguments by Israeli leftists and ultranationalists claiming his sentence was excessive and that he'd served far longer than other U.S. prisoners accused of similar crimes, arguments dismissed by previous administrations, which she prayed this president would also do.

"This can't be happening," she muttered folding the paper and shoving it into her handbag.

Until that morning, Laura had been on a daily regimen of twenty milligrams of the antidepressant Celexa. When prescribing it, her doctor had cautioned he might double the dosage if it failed to eliminate or ease her anxieties. Happily, the single pill had been sufficient and for a while her nightmares had subsided as did the palpitations. But after several weeks they returned, along with a new heightened sense of helplessness, which she endured in silence, fearing an increased dosage would turn her into a zombie. Now, with today's news, that concern evaporated. Digging through her handbag, she retrieved her pills, spilled three into her palm, and gulped them down with her coffee. Leaning back against the cool plastic seat, she closed her eyes and waited for the calm she'd need to get through the day.

Feeling the medication kick in, she eased away from the table and ventured to her car. She drove stiff-armed and slowly. The sun was over the tree line when she reached the employee parking lot, but rather than joining the others filing past her, she remained behind the wheel eyes closed, regulating her breathing.

Not long after her uncle's death, Laura had launched her letter writing campaign figuring to even the score for Israel's attack on the *Liberty*. When the letters failed to provoke Kleinman's fellow inmates, she grew impatient and requested a transfer from the federal prison in Schuylkill, in northeast Pennsylvania, to Butner, where she might prompt one of her patients to do the job. She'd been at Butner going on three months now, and so far no one seemed interested in the pudgy traitor. If today's news was to be believed, time was running out.

It was after eight when she heard a gentle tapping on her window.

"You okay, Laura?" a concerned co-worker asked when she lowered the window. "You're lookin' a mite peaked," he said leaning down.

She blinked him into focus. "No. No. I'm fine," she replied, working her jaw. "Just felt a little woozy, is all. I'm okay now."

"Better let the doc take a look-see. Lotta stuff going around these days. You never know what those folks and their families bring in here," he said, nodding at the prison.

"I will," she replied. "You go on in. I'll be there shortly."

"You sure?"

She nodded. "No need to worry," she said, and

watched him amble away.

Minutes later, she was pushing herself onto the pavement and testing her legs. By the time she reached the clinic she'd made up her mind. If she couldn't persuade someone to kill Leo Kleinman she would do it herself.

EIGHT

I telephoned the Israeli embassy and was informed no one there was authorized to respond to my queries regarding Leo Kleinman. Yes, they were aware of his status as an inmate in the U.S. federal prison system and of Israel's granting him citizenship, but there were complications preventing them from addressing my inquiries. However, if I wished to pursue the matter I should contact a Mr. Jacob Goodman, who, it was explained, while not connected to the embassy, might be of assistance.

Goodman's office was on Wisconsin Avenue in Bethesda, across the street from the Hyatt Hotel, on the Metro line. I phoned and introduced myself.

"Glad to hear from you, Mr. Shore," he said, his tone suggesting he'd been expecting my call. "We should talk. How about tomorrow? Can you make it tomorrow?" And when I said I could, he replied. "Fine. You know Morton's Steakhouse in Bethesda? It's in the Hyatt."

"I know the Hyatt," I said.

"Good. See you at six thirty."

"Six thirty?"

"Too early?"

"I thought you were going to say lunch."

"You don't eat dinner?"

"Of course."

"Lunch is for business, Mr. Shore. This isn't business. We're talking about a person."

A person who is a traitor, I thought.

I arrived promptly. "I'm here to meet a Mr. Goodman," I told the maître d'.

"Yes. He's expecting you." His manner suggested Goodman was a regular here. "Right this way," he said, leading me to the only occupied table, a banquette in the center of the room.

Obviously, six thirty was too early for the Bethesda glitterati.

"Your guest has arrived, Mr. Goodman," the maître d' said before backing away.

Goodman rose to greet me. He was dressed impeccably in a slim cut, dark blue suit, a crisp white shirt showing an inch of monogramed French cuff, silk tie and gleaming shoes. I knew a few FBI agents who wore Brioni suits—though I could never figure out how they afforded them—and his was much finer than those.

"Good evening, Mr. Shore," he said, from behind warm gray eyes.

His sonorous telephone voice had fooled me. I was expecting someone more robust and younger. Instead, I found a slender, elderly man with thinning hair and hollow cheeks, whose public voice was now soft and familial.

An uncorked bottle of Pinot Noir sat on the table, some of it already poured into two wine glasses, along with a chilled bottle of Perrier mineral water. Once I was seated and we were alone, Goodman raised his glass. "*Mazel.*"

"Aren't we supposed to say *L'a Chaim*?"

"*L'a Chaim* is to life. Life we have. What we need is

luck."

"Then here's mazel to you, as well," I replied lifting mine.

He smiled. "Just *mazel* is enough."

I told him I couldn't recall having tasted such fine wine.

"I'm glad you like it. I believe it was Mr. Shakespeare who said, 'Good wine is a good familiar creature if it be well used.' Let us use this wine well by having it cleanse our palettes and, more importantly, make friends of strangers."

"I'll drink to that," I replied. "Do you know Leo Kleinman?"

"Who doesn't know Leo?" Then, spreading his hands, "To some he's a traitor, to others a patriot."

"Put me in the traitor column, Mr. Goodman. He stole massive amounts of vital military secrets and sold them."

"To Israel, I know. Because of him many former Soviet Jews are living in Israel, Jews who might not otherwise be alive. So perhaps we shouldn't judge him so harshly."

"There are many who would take issue with you." And when he raised an eyebrow, I said, "I'm thinking of those Soviets whose identities were revealed when the secrets they provided us were turned over to the Kremlin by Israel. Wouldn't you agree those men and women also deserved to live?"

"Who among us is perfect?" Goodman said. "According to some, the last perfect man to walk the earth they crucified. But enough about Leo Kleinman," he said, waving a manicured hand. "Let's eat and enjoy each other's company. Later we'll talk about Leo."

"As you wish, Mr. Goodman."

"Please. Enough with the Mr. Goodman. Call me Max."

"Not Jacob?"

"Forget Jacob. Friends call me Max, so you'll call me Max."

"All right, Max."

"And should I call you Jerzy?"

I considered suggesting Iceman, but dismissed the notion. "Jerzy is fine."

"Do you get much ribbing with that name? Jerzy Shore?" he said with an understanding expression.

"Not much now. When I was younger I did, which usually ended with someone getting a swollen eye or bloody nose. Sometimes both." He was nodding as I spoke. "In the early years it was usually one-sided, but then I gave as good as I got."

"I had a friend, a decent man. Marvin Lipschitz. A week didn't go by his phone didn't ring in the middle of the night. 'Hello. Is this Mr. Lipschitz?' Before he could answer, they'd say, 'If your lip shits, my ass talks.' And then they would laugh like it was a new joke and hang up. One day, some putz said it to him in person and Marvin nearly killed the fellow." He was shaking his head. "All those years. That pent up frustration. He exploded like a cannon. A man can take only so much. But that doesn't make him a bad man," he said, holding my gaze. "*Verstehst?*"

I understood perfectly. Jews had suffered greatly throughout history, often silently. So who could blame them for fighting back when given the opportunity? Which was what Goodman was telling me Leo Kleinman had done in his own perverse way. But Leo Kleinman had betrayed his country and, for me, that was unpardonable.

"What's your line of work, Max?" I asked, moving on.

"I'm retired. I used to be in the garment business.

You heard of Hart Shaffner Marx?"

"That was *your* company?"

"I should be so lucky. No. I owned a clothing line, which I sold to them. Sports clothes, accessories. It was a good business, quality merchandise, and they paid well for it. Then this whole China thing comes along and they changed the line. Out went my Italian silks and wools, replaced with cheap fabrics, cheaply made. The accessories, also junk. Now it's all tchotchkes. You know tchotchkes? It's the stuff in your house a burglar wouldn't steal."

By the time dinner was over, I knew enough about Jacob, aka Max, Goodman to fill a thimble. Whenever the conversation turned to him, he skillfully relayed an amusing anecdote that kept it moving, but never in his direction. All I was able to gather from this engaging octogenarian was that he was born and raised in the Bronx, that he had studied at either Harvard or Brandeis University, or not, that he had an eye for pretty women, and may have once been married to a show girl from New York's famous nightclub, The Latin Quarter, and is now either living with or married to a former model. He claimed to enjoy opera and theater, but judging from his choice of wine, and how thoroughly he consumed his filet mignon and twice baked potato made especially for him, followed by a double portion of chocolate mousse, I'd say his appreciation for fine things went beyond the arts.

Most of the tables around us were occupied and the decibel level had increased when coffee was served. Looking around, Goodman leaned in and, lowering his voice, asked, "So what can I do to help you help Leo Kleinman?"

"To start with, you can provide me with those threatening letters he's received."

"What a terrible thing. The poor man's locked away nearly thirty years and now he has to worry about some *meshugana* lunatic," he said. Then signaling the waiter, he told him, "Tell Rudolph to bring me my briefcase." A moment later, the maître d' delivered a thin black leather satchel, which he dutifully set beside Goodman.

"Here you are, Mr. Goodman," he said, and quickly departed.

"Do you think these will help find the person?" he asked, unsnapping the catch and reaching inside. "We've studied them, but they tell us little about the author."

"Who's *we*, Max?"

He shrugged. "Friends of Leo," he said, handing over a large manila envelope containing what looked to be a dozen or so unsigned letters of varying length.

"It's possible," I said. "With so little to go on, any lead will help. You've talked with Kleinman about these?"

"Others have, but he is unable to provide any information."

I wondered who the *others* were, possibly the Mossad. "Mind if I take a quick look?" I asked.

"Look!" he said before excusing himself and heading to the men's room.

He was gone long enough for me to give them a quick read. When he still hadn't returned, I looked around and saw him in close conversation with a woman, whose back was to me. They were across the room, in an alcove, and when he caught me looking his way, he raised a finger indicating he would return momentarily. When I looked over again, she was gone.

"So what did you discover?" he asked nodding at the letters as he slid into his seat.

"Probably not much more than you and your team did. I'd like to know what the link is between the writer and the Israeli attack on the USS *Liberty*."

"*Mistaken attack*," Goodman corrected.

I couldn't resist. "That was a helluva mistake. Thirty-four dead. One hundred seventy-one wounded."

He shrugged.

"Discovering a *Liberty* link would help," I said. "A search your folks no doubt already conducted."

"It was looked into, but without success. You Navy investigators are better suited for such an investigation."

"Thanks for the vote of confidence. Did your people come up with anything conclusive?"

"The writer's a woman."

"Really?" I said, examining the letters again. "How'd they arrive at that?"

"They had some linguistic experts study them."

"How can they be sure?"

Another shrug. "What do I know from linguistics? You'll have to ask your experts."

"I will," I assured him.

"So when are you going to see Leo?" he asked as we were leaving.

"Probably in a day or two," I said. "I'll call down and get on his visitors' list."

"Good. Tell him Max said hello."

* * *

I spent the following morning at the FBI's Behavioral Research and Instruction Unit in Quantico, with one of their forensic linguistics, who confirmed what Goodman had told me. From the BRIU I went to see Scully, my boss.

"Good afternoon, love of my life," I said to Miss Personality.

"He's busy. You should have called ahead," she

replied with a thin smile, while barely glancing my way.

"Tell him I'm here about the Kleinman case," I said, stroking one of her Beanie Babies.

"These are not toys," she said, snatching it and setting it with the others on the credenza behind her. Then, turning to her intercom, she rang Scully and asked, "Are you free to see Agent Shore about the Kleinman case?"

When I heard him say, "Send him in," I strode past her and said, "That's Special Agent."

"There's nothing special about you," she countered.

"Afternoon, Chief," I said as I entered.

"What've you got?" He was in his usual end-of-the-day sour mood.

Ah, the curse of the uninitiated, I mused, while trying to ignore the negative chi swirling around us. One day he'll thank me for converting this hell hole into a positive life force environment, I told myself as I slid the chair before his desk to a more hospitable spot. Sadly, this wasn't the day.

"Looks like the letter writer is a woman who's somehow affiliated with the USS *Liberty*."

"Affiliated in what way?"

Spreading out the letters, I showed him the key words and phrases circled in red pencil. "I don't know yet. The reference to the ship doesn't necessarily mean there's a family connection, but it's a starting point."

"How do you know it's a woman?" He didn't sound convinced.

"The folks at BRIU did a content analysis and, based on the writing style and language, they're certain. Look here," I said, indicating the highlighted areas. "Females use more punctuation than males, and when they do, they tend to insert multiple punctuation marks. They also frequently express feelings and use enhancing qualifiers and adverbs. Plus, there's the recurring use of the word 'love,' another female trait. They use more quotation marks around words than men do, and they express their feelings more often and more candidly. Finally, using the script font, she signs the letters *anonymous*. Another giveaway. Men don't do that. They simply leave it blank." The red circles were jumping off the pages at us.

"Also, judging from her grammar, they believe she likely hasn't gone much further than high school."

When I concluded, we both agreed it was time I paid a visit to Butner. On the way to my office I stopped by Theo's and dropped off copies of the letters, hoping he might find a link between the woman and the *Liberty*.

NINE

Ruth altered her routine on her next visit to Butner. Departing Bethesda Wednesday rather than Monday, and checking into The Inn at Creedmoor instead of the Best Western, where she usually stayed because of its indoor pool, fitness center, and ten percent discount for prison visitors. She also skipped dinner at Bob's Barbeque, opting instead for Pergamon's, where she arrived wearing a tailored summer outfit.

She stood inside the entrance beside the *Please Wait to be Seated* sign until the young waitress appeared, then followed her into the dining room, shoulders squared, looking neither left nor right, her pointed heels clicking sharply on the parquet floor.

"These are our specials," the girl told her, pausing before the chalkboard set on an easel. "I recommend the chicken gorgonzola. It's to die for."

"Sounds interesting," she said, and followed her to a table that placed her in everyone's view.

"Will this be all right, ma'am?" the waitress asked.

"I prefer a booth," she replied, her eyes sweeping the half-full room. "That one," she said, nodding at the unoccupied table beneath the large mural depicting the ancient Greek city of Pergamon, and across from the man she had seen with Goodman at Mortons.

"Something to drink?" she was asked when seated.

"Makers Mark perfect Manhattan, straight up," she said, adjusting her skirt, while exchanging glances with the man.

She was three bites into her meal when a patron from the bar wandered over and slid in opposite her without invitation.

"Couldn't help noticing you're about ready for a second one," he said setting his glass down and nodding at hers. "Okay if I order you one?"

"Thank you, but I'm fine," she replied, averting his gaze.

"You sure are, honey."

"Look," she said, in a firm tone, "I'm not your honey, and I prefer dining alone, if you don't mind."

He waved a hand. "I ain't here to eat. Just looking to have a friendly drink, is all. You go on ahead with your dinner, and I'll just order us a round and keep you company," he said, signaling the waitress.

Ruth set her fork down. "Please. Forget the drink and kindly leave."

Heads were turning and conversations pausing.

"Hey. I'm just being neighborly. You look like you could use some company and…"

"If I wanted company," she said, "it wouldn't be with the likes of you. Now, beat it, you pathetic clown."

His smile fell away. "Pathetic clown! Where do you get off talkin' to me like that?" he said shoving the table and sending her drink onto her.

"You sonofabitch!" she cried.

In the next instant, he was yanked from his seat and thrown to the floor, sprawled there with Jerzy pinning him with his foot. A woman across the room shrieked, sending the waitress scampering into the kitchen.

"You're way outta line, fella," Jerzy said, his no-nonsense voice filling the still room.

"Get off," the man cried. "My back."

Jerzy was telling him to stop squirming and to cool down, when the kitchen door flew open, ejecting a bear of a man who came at them with flared nostrils and clenched fists.

"Goddamn troublemakers!" the burly owner yelled, tearing off his apron and lunging at Jerzy. "Gonna give you a real taste of trouble," he said, grabbing Jerzy's jacket and drawing his fist back.

"Whoa, Robby!" someone called from a nearby table. "Twas the guy on the bottom started it," he said, jumping up and coming over. "Saw the whole thing. This un," he said, indicating the one on the floor, "insulted the lady, and spilled a drink on her to boot. This fella did what any gentleman woulda done. No telling what might've happened if he hadn't stepped in."

The owner listened without taking his eyes from Jerzy. And, while he seemed unconvinced, he allowed his fist to come down slowly.

"That's exactly how it happened," the man's wife assured him from her seat.

Still holding onto Jerzy, who offered no resistance, he assessed the scene, and asked, "Whatta you got to say?"

"It's like the gentleman said. This joker was bothering the lady. Came over uninvited, and when she told him to scram things got messy, and I couldn't allow that."

"It's true," Ruth said, her voice cracking. "I'm here for a quiet dinner, minding my own business and this… this jerk comes over and …"

"No need to cry, ma'am," the owner said gently now, his scowl receding.

"I'm not crying, damn it!" she said wiping away tears. "I'm angry."

Releasing Jerzy, the owner said, "Let him up." Then, grabbing a fistful of the man's shirt, he pulled him close, and said, "This ain't no juke joint, mister. You hear me?"

"I... I didn't think it was."

"Then why you acting like it is?"

"Didn't mean to. Honest."

"You ain't from around here," said the owner.

"No. Just passing through," the man said, eyeing the men now pressing in around them. "Really, I didn't mean no harm. Things sorta got outta hand."

"Maybe he ought to pass through our jail," someone suggested.

"Should I call the sheriff, Robby?" another asked.

"No need for that," the man replied when it appeared the owner was considering the idea. Then, twisting under the owner's grasp, he turned to Ruth as best he could and said, "I'm sorry, Miss. I truly am." And, to the owner, "If it's okay," he said, reaching for his wallet, "I'd like to pay for the cleaning. This should cover it," he said pulling out a twenty and placing it on the table.

"What about her meal?" someone prompted. "Oughta pay for that, too."

"Yeah, right," he said, dropping down three tens.

"Don't forget the tip," the owner said, finally releasing him. "Waitress has to clean up this mess."

"How's this?" he said, adding a five, and then another when that didn't seem to satisfy him.

"That'll do," the owner said.

"I'm sorry for the trouble," he told the owner. And to Ruth, who was dabbing at her clothes with her napkin, "I'm sorry, Miss."

"I ever see you in here again," the owner said, "you're gonna find out what real trouble is. You got that?"

"I got it," he said, his head bobbing.

Now, you best leave, before I forget this is a family

restaurant."

Shoving his wallet into his pocket, the man replied, "I'm on my way." Easing his way through the knot of men around him, he hurried to the door without looking back.

"And don't come back," someone called.

Once everyone had returned to their tables, the owner apologized to Ruth, repeating this was a family restaurant, that nothing like this ever happens, and would she consider staying while he prepared a fresh meal? "Please," he implored. "I don't want you going away angry."

She looked around, sighed, and said, "I suppose."

"You're welcome to join me," Jerzy offered. "I promise to behave."

"Good idea," the owner said. "And I'll fix you both a nice dinner."

"Haven't I caused you enough trouble?" she told Jerzy.

"No trouble at all. I'd welcome the company."

She considered the invitation. "I'll need to straighten up first."

"Take your time," he said.

Together, he and the owner watched her head for the restroom, their gaze lingering on her.

When she returned, there was a fresh drink at her place.

* * *

I had just started on my chicken gorgonzola when the room went silent. Glancing up, I saw her in the entryway waiting to be seated. She was a dream. Tall, shapely and smartly dressed, she was a knockout. Even the women were staring, but without the hungry look of their companions. I watched her approach the menu board, seemingly unaware of the attention she was generating, and was pleased when she chose a table closer to mine than the one offered her. And when she looked my way, I felt my face warm.

I was certain someone would be joining her once he parked the car, and was surprised when the waitress set down one menu and cleared away the extra place setting. A woman like that shouldn't be dining alone, I thought, while enjoying the brief view of her thigh as she slid into the booth.

With the two of us the only singles in the room, and encouraged by her occasional glances my way, I pondered inviting her to join me. But I waited too long. Her meal arrived, and with it a missed opportunity.

Sitting there toying with my food, I considered several opening gambits, all hinging on making eye contact again. And when that didn't happen, I thought of simply asking if she'd be open to joining me for an after-dinner drink at the bar. But even then I was too late. The fella I'd spotted staring into his glass at the bar earlier was off his stool and making his move. He was greasy looking and, unless I misjudged her, not her type. This isn't going to go well, I thought, setting down my fork.

I looked around. No one seemed aware of what was about to happen, including the woman herself. That is, until he slid in across from her, offering a toothy smile. And, while I couldn't hear his opening line, I did catch her response. Things went downhill from there, and I smiled inwardly when he spilled her drink. It was time for the Iceman to intervene.

* * *

George Vercessi

"Sorry to keep you waiting," she said, when returning from the ladies' room, "but I wanted to wash the liquor out of my dress before it set in."

She had also brushed her hair and applied fresh lip gloss. A good sign.

Raising her glass, she said, "To my hero. You handled the situation admirably. Thank you for coming to my aid."

"All in a knight's work. That's knight with a k."

"And what does this shining knight do when he isn't rescuing damsels?"

"You familiar with the TV show *NCIS*?"

"You're a television producer?"

"No. I'm one of them."

"Oh. An actor."

I shook my head. "I'm an NCIS agent."

Tilting her head, she asked, "So why did you mention the television show?"

This wasn't going well. I took a sip of my drink, and said, "I shouldn't have."

"But you did."

"It was meant as a shortcut, but obviously not a very effective one. I figured since most folks know the show I wouldn't have to explain what NCIS is. You know, eliminate the details and keep the conversation flowing. Like if I said, 'I'm an FBI agent.' Say it, get it out of the way and move on."

She was shaking her head. "But you're *not* an FBI agent."

"Right. I'm not an FBI age... Wait a second! You're putting me on."

She grinned. "Had you going there. But be honest, you were bragging. Linking yourself to that show."

I shrugged. "You caught me."

Reaching out, she brushed my hand. "You're entitled.

The way you stepped up and took care of that boorish man. No one's ever done anything like that for me. And between you and me, you're better looking than what's his name—the star of that show."

"Mark Harmon."

In the next instant, she was asking to see my badge, and when I passed over my wallet, she studied my ID, and returned it with a frown.

"Something wrong?" I asked.

But she didn't say. Instead, she asked, "What brings you to Butner, Special Agent Shore?"

I was expecting an inane comment about my name, like most folks make when we first meet, and I was pleased when it didn't come. "Jerzy is fine."

"And I'm Sarah," she said with a warm smile. "So, Jerzy, are you passing through, or here on business?"

"Business."

"That's it, nothing more, just *business*?" When I nodded, she offered a knowing smile. Leaning in, she whispered, "I get it. You're on a secret mission. Okay. I can go with that."

"Nothing so dramatic," I assured her. "Just a routine case. What about you?" I asked, feeling I was back in the speed dating scene. "Live here or passing through?"

She pursed her lips and considered the question. "I live in Maryland, but I'm a frequent visitor."

"Business or pleasure?"

She shrugged. "A little of both."

"Care to elaborate?"

"Maybe after a few more of these," she said, tapping her empty glass.

"In that case," I said, signaling the waitress.

The meal forgotten, we soon finished our drinks and moved on to another round and then another. Nestled in that booth, in the glow of her dark chocolate eyes and warm smile, I was soon babbling on about the benefits of feng shui, the hassle of tending to an ailing older sister, my early career chasing down domestic abusers and my current duties in the cold case squad. To my delight, she appeared genuinely interested.

When the conversation eventually turned to her, she explained that she was visiting someone at Butner—without saying who—a journey she made twice a month.

"How long have you been coming here?" I asked.

"A number of years."

"That's quite a commitment," I said, hoping to learn more.

She shrugged. "Sometimes there are things you have to do."

We were ready for another round, and when I waved the waitress over she informed us it was closing time.

I looked around. We were the only ones in the place. "What time do you close?" I asked checking my watch. It was ten fifteen.

"We close at ten."

"So early?"

"We don't hardly get much call for dinner at this hour," she said.

I apologized for keeping her beyond closing time, and left an extra-large tip. As we stood to leave, the owner came over and asked if there was something wrong with the meal, since we had returned it barely touched. We told him it was delicious, but we were too wound up from the incident earlier to enjoy it.

"No problem," he said. "Next time, dinner's on the house."

The parking lot held only two cars. "Which one's yours?" I asked.

"Neither," she replied. "Didn't drive. Where's

yours?"

"Walked. I'm staying over there," I said indicating the Creedmoor across the street.

She leaned into me and said, "How convenient. So am I."

"Mind if I walk you home?" I asked.

"Love it."

We linked arms and walked a bit unsteadily across the gravel lot. When we reached the hotel, I looked into those dark eyes, and said, "This has been an incredible evening."

She smiled. "Aren't you going to see me to my room, Agent Shore?"

TEN

Laura had made up her mind. Today she'd cross the line and ignore the Fellowship of the Badge by consorting with the enemy. In doing so, she'd be disregarding institutional training and the rules governing relations between staff and inmates. She had considered the matter carefully. Breaking trust with the institution and prison staff was not only a crime, it also set her up to be extorted by the very inmates she was attempting to manipulate. Yet, she felt she had no choice. Kleinman could not be allowed to go free, even if it meant confiding in men with little or nothing to lose, men wanting to do time their way, with their rules, and who were masters at manipulating others.

After passing through security, Laura deposited her cell phone and purse in her locker and changed into her uniform. She had not applied perfume, makeup or nail polish today, and her hair, usually worn below her shoulders, was tied back in a severe bun. There would be nothing to offend or distract her first patient during their twenty minutes together; twenty minutes ostensibly to clean his teeth while focusing the conversation on the traitor Leo Kleinman.

Jamal Rasheed (née Javon Roberts) grew up on the

rough streets of Wilmington, Delaware. Small in stature, Javon was quick with his mouth if not his fists. Opting out of high school, the fatherless teenager ran with a loose crew of similar misfits, who, like Javon, thought they knew it all, until they were swept up in a guns-for-drugs dragnet that subsequently earned them long prison terms. Now twenty-five, this radicalized Muslim, having recently transferred to Camp Fluffy from the cell blocks in Butner's medium II facility, was serving out the short end of a mandatory ten-year sentence.

Prior to his conviction, Javon had spurned advice, particularly the type intended to steer him away from the trouble he eventually landed in; but that changed upon entering the federal prison system. "Join up if you want to survive," a brother had cautioned soon after he stepped inside. Looking around, Javon saw the hostility in the faces of his fellow inmates and, determining the brother knew what he was talking about, promptly signed on with the Black Muslims. To his surprise, he liked their structured life—the daily prayers, eating no pork, and placing trust in the prophet Mohammed's teachings—and soon, he was openly championing the merits of an Islamic state and Sharia law.

"You new?" he asked as he strutted into Laura's cubicle, hands swinging low beside his hips, eyes drifting over her lose-fitting green scrubs. "I ain't seen you before."

Laura looked up from his chart. "I've been here about two months. Transferred down from Schuykill. Outside Minersville."

"Yeah. I know the place. Got some brothers freezin' their black asses up there," he said, sliding into the chair and swinging his legs up like he owned the place, while being careful not to cross his legs, lest he spoil the knife edge in his starched uniform.

"It does get pretty cold up there," she agreed. "I was happy to get away."

"You'll like it better here." After raising his chin, to allow Laura to fasten the paper bib around his neck, he asked, "So, tell me. How come I be on today's Call Out sheet? It ain't four months since I been here." He wasn't complaining. Rather, he was happy for any screw-up in the system that pulled him out of his kitchen duties. Any break in routine was good, especially when it brought him close to a woman, even if she wasn't pretty.

"I was looking over your chart, Javon," she said, using his first name, a breach in protocol she was certain did not go unnoticed. "And I see we hadn't completed your prophylactic treatment during your last visit."

Roberts shot up, his feet landing flat on the floor. "The hell, you say! I ain't got no damn mouth disease."

"No," she said resting her hand on his shoulder and gently pressing him back into the chair and leaving it there, in another procedural violation. "You don't have any issues," she said with a reassuring smile.

"Then what's this prolactic business? You thinkin' 'bout testin' some shit on me, forget it. 'Cause it ain't happenin'. You got that?"

"Prophylactic treatment prevents infection and gum disease and keeps the teeth strong," she said, bringing over his chart, the one she had altered. "See? This section isn't filled in, which means you didn't receive a fluoride treatment when you were here last. That's all."

"Yeah, I know fluoride. Never heard of that prolactic, though."

"It won't take long."

"Too bad," he said, eyeing her breasts. "I wouldn't mind it takin' a hour or two."

"I'm sure you wouldn't. And since you're in no hurry, I'll give your teeth another scraping and polishing as long as you're here. Give you a nice healthy smile."

"Yeah. That's what I need in here, a healthy smile. Maybe they'll make me warden with my healthy smile. By the way, the name's Jamal Rasheed."

"Rasheed?" She looked at his record again. "Says Javon. Javon Roberts here."

"I don't care what it say. It's Jamal Rasheed to the brothers. And that's how it's gonna be when I'm outta this stinkin' hole. So, you don't mind, call me by my rightful name."

"Did you convert to Islam?"

"Yeah. That's right. I converted. I'm a practicin' Muslim now. You got that?"

Laura smiled beneath her face mask. She got it all right, which is why he was sitting there before her. "Jamal Rasheed," she said, drawing out the name. "Strong name. It suits you."

"Yeah," he said with a smug grin, his eyes flashing. "Suits me fine. Gonna be a whole new life once I'm outside."

Laura slipped on a pair of Latex gloves, retrieved her tools and rolled her chair over—her breasts against his arm, he instantly pressing back—and, with the stem mirror and curette, she began scraping his lower molars. "So, Jamal," she said, staying with his first name, "you been following what's going on over in Gaza? That fighting between your Muslim brothers and the Israelis?"

"Yah," he managed, while nodding.

"Poor Palestinians aren't asking for much," she said, "only some land to call their own." He grunted and nodded again, while she went on, grieving over the casualties and widespread destruction, her mouth close to his ear, her voice soft but insistent. "I know a woman whose parents' apartment was bombed. Totally destroyed. Last she heard, they were living in a tent somewhere among the rubble, scrounging for food."

He reached over, pretending to scratch his elbow, allowing his fingers to linger against her breast and keeping them there when she didn't object.

"It's just horrible what those poor, innocent Muslims have to endure," she continued. "No place is safe. Even the hospitals are being attacked, and those still standing can barely handle half the wounded. So many women and children. I've seen pictures—the schools, the water and power plants—all targeted." She paused, the implements still in his mouth, her eyes meeting his. "It's heartbreaking how Israel treats those people, fencing in nearly two million Muslims on a strip of land five miles wide. It's like a prison." Her nipple grew hard against his slim fingers.

"I've heard Gaza called the largest prison in the world," she said. "No wonder so many folks hate Americans. The way Israel draws us into their messes. Some allies. Now, you take Leo Kleinman over in Clemson unit. You know him?"

He gave a curt nod.

"All those military secrets he sold to Israel. Our secrets. Think they returned them when we caught him, those great allies of ours?" She paused. "Nuh-uh. Gave them to the Soviets instead. Gave them our secrets. Then, if that ain't bad enough, they made Kleinman a citizen. The little kike gets an Israeli passport and a fat paycheck every month he's here, to be collected when he gets out. Can you beat that?"

"Whaa?" he mumbled. And when she removed the instruments from his mouth, "You jokin'. That Jew motherfucker's getting' paid?" he said, careful not to move his hand.

She nodded while reinserting the scraper. "Money

is deposited in his Israeli bank account every month. Going on thirty years, now. They say he's a millionaire. Thinking I'll have to work on him one of these days makes my blood boil. Don't know why he wasn't executed," she said, extracting her implements and pushing her stool away. "Okay, Jamal. Go ahead and rinse."

He swished, spit out and wiped his chin with his sleeve. "What you mean he be gettin' out?"

"Says in the papers. The president's thinking of pardoning him. Freeing the traitor so he can live the life of a millionaire over there, where they're killing those poor Muslims. Sometimes I wish I had a gun."

"How soon?"

Laura shrugged. "End of the year the way they're talking, maybe sooner," she said, placing the instruments in the cassette to be sterilized later. "Sure would be nice if something happened to him before then. That would be justice."

"There's a mess of Jews in here," he said. "Maybe they should all be shot."

"He's the only traitor," she reminded him. "The others haven't sold out their country."

He squinted. "Ain't how I hear it. Everybody knows they run this country. Got the top payin' jobs, while keepin' the brothers and sisters down. Wouldn't be a bad idea to ice the lot of 'em."

"Someone could do this country a big favor if they took care of just this one," she said.

"Not much chance of that. Still…" he fell silent, his gaze drifting off somewhere in the middle distance before going to the paper cup in his hand. Looking up, he crumpled the cup and tossed it in the wastebasket beside him. "Sure would be nice drinkin' out of a real glass stead of the plastic ones they give us. Know what

I'm gonna do first thing I get out? Eat a meal off some real dishes, stead of that plastic shit they give us, and use a real knife and fork, too. And drink cold beer from a glass," he said, smacking his lips as if downing the icy brew.

"Like this one?" Laura said removing her drinking glass from the cabinet and handing it to him.

"Yeah," he said, caressing it. "'Cept this one's chipped."

"Really? Where?"

"Right here," he said handing it back.

"Time to get a new one," she said, dropping it in the wastebasket. Then, turning away, she brought out her pen and updated his chart. "Probably a good idea, Jamal, to have you back for a set of x-rays. You haven't had any for some time," she said over her shoulder.

"You think so?" he said, his eyes falling to her round ass. "How soon?"

She turned and smiled. "Depends on when I can fit you in. Maybe a week or so."

When she emptied the wastebasket later the glass was gone.

ELEVEN

What's up, man?" the elderly black inmate asked Rasheed, finding him crouched behind a row of shrubs pressing something into the soft soil with the heel of his shoe.

"Don't concern you, nigga. Now get away 'fore some rat gets wonderin' and we all go into lockdown."

"You got hooch?" the man said, his eyes widening. "'Cause if'n you do, you know the rules. No hooch for Muslims. And you bein' one, you can't be drinkin' that stuff. You know what I'm sayin'?"

Rasheed, came away from the building and paused before starting back toward the kitchen. "I know exactly what you sayin', old man, and there ain't no hooch. And if it was, I wouldn't be sharin' it with the likes of you." Then, cracking his knuckles, he said, "You be smart, you stay away from behind them bushes and keep your black mouth shut, you know what's good for you. Or you be takin' your meals with a straw. Know what *I'm sayin'*?"

The man rubbed his gray stubble as if recalling a similar run-in and shuffled off without comment.

Rasheed, in turn, headed for the kitchen with several shards from the broken drinking glass he'd just buried, the slivers concealed in a torn dish rag stuffed in his pocket. These he'd grind up in the shower, one of the few places in the prison where he had privacy. When the time came, he'd mix the glass with Kleinman's food. As a kitchen worker, he knew the mess hall routine; knew inmates ate quickly so as not to keep others waiting. Knowing the Jews checked in with the guard before claiming their kosher meals, he'd be ready when Kleinman came through the line.

But that wasn't enough. Before targeting Kleinman, he had to study him carefully—noting how he proceeded through the chow line, how carefully or carelessly he opened the sealed kosher meal, and how he ate it, with whom and if he shared it. Rasheed wanted to know if he played with his food or shoveled it into his mouth. Did he gulp it down or take small bites? These were things he believed he needed to know. He wasn't leaving anything to chance.

Rasheed smiled when he spotted Kleinman with the guard, his yarmulke-covered head bobbing as he checked in. *Come on, Jew boy. Come get your meal.*

"Yo!" the inmate standing before Rasheed, snarled. "I ain't got all day."

Rasheed turned to the burly con hovering over him and wordlessly scooped a helping of rice and beans onto his plate, less than what he'd have doled out to a brother, knowing the white cracker wouldn't complain, since it worked in reverse when whites and Latinos served their own.

"Kosher," Kleinman announced when reaching the head of the line, his attention diverted to a distant table where his Jewish comrades were gathered, looking to see if a place would soon be available.

Smiling inward, Rasheed retrieved the prepackaged meal and passed it to him. *Gonna die soon, motherfucker.*

* * *

Laura was sleep-deprived when leaving for work. This time, after watching Al Jazeera's television documentary, *The Day Israel Attacked the United States*, the previous night. Not even a double dose of antidepressant eased her tremors that morning. Seeing aging *Liberty* crewmembers, men she knew from numerous *Liberty* reunions, recounting events of that fatal day had sent her into a tailspin. She'd trembled hearing them describe feeling secure that calm morning under the watchful eyes of an ally—they had counted eight Israeli reconnaissance planes dipping low, their pilots waving as they circled the ship before the unprovoked attack.

When first seeing the show's promos, she considered skipping it, avoiding it entirely. She knew the survivors' stories, had heard them recount where on the ship they had been that day. She'd also read many of their accounts in books and articles. Yet she was drawn to the program, wanting to be certain Al Jazeera portrayed the assault accurately, not as an unfortunate accident, as Israel maintains, but as a deliberate attack.

To its credit, Al Jazeera allowed crewmembers to speak freely and without interruption. Refusing to be silenced, *Liberty's* survivors gave convincing testimony that never made it into the Navy's official investigation, testimony clearly demonstrating Israel's intent to sink the ship. They spoke, too, of Sixth Fleet aircraft launched to defend them, but recalled by President Johnson, and the despair they felt at being abandoned.

Tears streamed down Laura's cheeks as distraught sailors told of deafening explosions, and armor-piercing shells ripping their shipmates apart, and of the torpedo attack that tossed their ship like a cork and snuffed out so many lives below deck. She sobbed when they expressed their fear the ship was about to sink and seeing their lifeboats riddled with bullets from Israeli torpedo boats.

But most distressing, were the personal accounts of life after the attack—of broken families, rampant alcoholism, bouts of depression, and post-traumatic stress, not unlike Laura observed while caring for her uncle.

Had it not been for Kleinman's pending release, she would have called in sick that morning. But with that possibility looming, she was compelled to take her plan to the next step. If the horny Muslim who'd caressed her breast wasn't up to the task, she was hoping the tattooed skinhead she'd scheduled that morning might be.

Her eyes fell to the twin SS Nazi lightning bolts inked onto the fold of skin between his right thumb and forefinger and she hoped he hadn't noticed her trembling hands as she placed the bib around his thick neck, partially covering the swastika below his ear. She had been in the prison system long enough to know the red circled AB letters on his forearm announced his membership in the white supremacist Aryan Brotherhood that lived by the motto *Blood In/Blood Out*, signifying the requirement for membership was killing a black man, and quitting meant death. She knew, too, that as one of the nation's largest prison gangs, the AB was responsible for a quarter of the murders in the federal prison system, which was another reason for approaching him. She had known members while at Schuylkill, and found them articulate and polite. She hoped the same was true at Butner.

"How are you today, Mr. Chatham?" she asked the clean-shaven young man.

"Much better now," he replied with a pleasant air. "Nothing like being in the company of a fine-looking woman to raise one's morale. And how are you doing, ma'am?"

She had applied color to her face and brushed out her hair, confident it wouldn't offend him, as it might the Muslim calling himself Rasheed. But there was little she could do to mask her tired, puffy eyes.

"I'd have to say I could be better," she said steadying her hands. And when he offered a puzzled look, she added, "Just frustrated, is all."

He laughed. "Aren't we all. If I might be so bold as to inquire, what seems to be bothering you?"

She licked her dry lips. "It's the spy over in Clemson — Kleinman."

"You mean Doughboy. That's what we call him. Little fat guy with a beard and glasses." Then, raising an eyebrow, he asked, "He giving you trouble?"

"No, not directly. I'm upset because there's talk he's about to be released."

"Doughboy's getting out?"

"The papers say the president may grant him clemency."

"Don't believe those stories," he said, waving his hand. "They make that stuff up."

"Maybe so, but not this time. Not from what I've been reading," she said. "Knowing how much the Israelis want him, the president's planning to use Kleinman to get them to make concessions to the Palestinians in the peace talks."

He shook his head. "That's nonsense, Kleinman's a nobody."

"He may be nobody here," she countered, "but he's a hero over there."

"They're addicted to conflict over there. The negotiations aren't going anywhere, and neither is Doughboy," he assured her.

Wanting to believe him, she said, "What makes you so sure?"

For the next few minutes Chatham gave her a brief tutorial on the peace talks, their origin, pitfalls, why they were stalled, and why they were set up to fail. "You know," he said, "the U.N. offered the Jews and Palestinians their own independent state. The Israelis accepted the plan, the Palestinians didn't. That should tell you something."

Laura stepped back. "I'm impressed. How do you know so much?"

Chatham offered an understanding smile. "Don't let the tats fool you, ma'am. We're not all Neanderthals. I have an undergraduate degree and a masters in international relations." And when Laura blinked, he said with a short laugh, "Unfortunately, they weren't enough to keep me out of prison."

Feeling foolish, she asked, "So, you don't believe the president's offer'll motivate them?"

He shrugged. "Anything's possible. More likely he's dangling Doughboy out there to gauge how far he can move them in the negotiations."

"And if they signal the right response," she said, her stomach knotting, "he'll be free?"

"I don't think they will. Not this prime minister."

After a moment, she said, "You realize he's an Israeli citizen with a big bank account waiting for him?"

Chatham was enjoying the discussion. It was a welcome diversion from the usual prison banter. But he wasn't certain why they were having it. As a staff member, this woman had the leverage and authority of a correction officer; in fact, technically, she was a CO, which meant she could be setting him up for something that would put him at risk, both with the AB and the prison. "Why are you telling me this?"

"Because you asked what was bothering me."

"So I did. And the notion of Doughboy's release somehow bothers you?" And when she nodded, he asked, "Why him?"

"Well..., he's a traitor and he deserves to die in here. Just like those Walker brothers—the ones who sold Navy secrets to the Soviets. Why should he get off because he sold them to Israel, who traded them for Russian Jews?"

"Israel's a unique ally. They're surrounded by enemies who want them dead."

Laura forced a laugh. "Allies don't attack each other!"

He blinked. "When did that happen?"

Laura busied herself unwrapping her instruments, placing them on the tray in a slow, deliberate manner. And when he repeated the question, she turned and replied, "Before you were born. They tried sinking one of our ships during the Six-Day War. Attacked it without warning or provocation. Does that sound like an ally?"

Chatham rubbed his chin. "You sure about that?"

"I guess you didn't study that in school."

He shook his head. "No, I didn't."

"USS *Liberty*. One hundred-seventy-one injured, thirty-four dead. They claim it was a mistake, but it wasn't."

He didn't respond. After a moment, he asked, "Did they say when he would be released?"

"No. But it sounds like it might be soon. Unless..."

"Unless what?"

Swinging the tray over and rolling her chair beside him, she said, "Unless he's dead. Now open wide."

TWELVE

I opened one eye. The sun was barely up, and I pulled the blanket to my shoulder, intending to sleep a bit longer.

"You awake?" Sarah asked, rolling toward me, her hand sliding below the covers. "Oh, you're awake, all right," she said taking hold of me. "Wanna play?"

"Must we?"

"What's the matter, cowboy?"

"Is there no satisfying you, woman?" I mumbled through a dry mouth.

She laughed. "Don't hoot with the owls at night, if you can't fly with the eagles in the morning."

The next instant she was straddling me. Given my hangover, I surprised myself and, I think, Sarah as well. When we finished, we were both sweating and breathing heavily.

"Have enough?" I asked.

She slid off me. "Never enough."

"Surely, you can't mean that."

Coming up on one elbow, she leaned in and asked, "Is it a sin to enjoy making love?"

"I guess that depends."

"On what?"

"On your religion. What's yours?"

"What if I don't have one?" she said before moving away and heading for the bathroom, stepping over a trail of clothes torn off earlier, while providing a delicious view of her dimpled bottom that had me thinking she was right about not getting enough. Soon the shower was running. "You coming in?" she called.

"On my way," I shouted, springing from the bed, which is when I felt the full effect of my hangover and, hating to admit it, my age. Steadying myself against a chair, I looked around for a bottle of water, and seeing only my profile in the mirror immediately resolved to diet and exercise more. Minutes later, I was being lathered with expert hands, and with Sarah working her magic on me, all thoughts of self-improvement were forgotten.

We parted soon after breakfast, but not before promising to meet later for dinner. With time to spare before my appointment with the warden, I checked in with Theo back at the office.

"How's the search going?" I asked.

He laughed. "Do you have any idea of the scope of this quest?"

I cleared my throat, and conceded, "I have a general idea."

"Well, Iceman, lemme see if I can help you understand the problem. Of the thirty-four killed, twenty-five left widows, which we're trying to locate. As you might guess, a number of them remarried, some more than once. If none of them is your letter writer, we'll widen the net to include children, sisters, aunts and cousins. This isn't going to be easy, even with the extra help the chief assigned to the job. By the way, you got a lot of fence-mending to do when this wraps up. Folks don't appreciate being pulled off their cases."

With my head still throbbing I didn't want to think about it. "I'll worry about that later."

But Theo wasn't through. "After we finish with the families of the deceased, we'll look at families of the one hundred-seventy one injured crewmen. I imagine Kleinman'll be dead before we finish with them. But, if he isn't, there's also the rest of the crew's families to track down."

Theo usually put a positive spin on things, but there was nothing encouraging about this assessment. "Doesn't sound good," I said.

He chuckled. "Don't lose faith. Maybe we'll get lucky and find our gal in the first batch. How're you making out?"

I hadn't expected the question and I laughed.

"What's so funny?"

Thinking of Sarah, I was tempted to say, "My luck's finally changed." Instead, I said, "Nothing. I'm meeting with the warden today, and later with Kleinman. I'll let you know what I learn."

I arrived at Butner twenty minutes early, parked in the empty visitor lot, and walked to the admin building. The place was strangely quiet.

"I'm here to see the warden," I told the guard, handing over my ID and badge. "I have a ten o'clock appointment."

The guard, a crew cut kid, early twenties, pressed uniform, studied the ID and fingered the badge. "NCIS. Like the TV show," he said.

"Not exactly. We don't solve cases in an hour."

"Have you met Mark Harmon, the show's star?" he asked, and then looked disappointed when I shook my head. "How do you become an NCIS agent? I've been wanting to get into federal law enforcement."

"You are," I reminded him.

He shook his head. "I don't mean BOP. I want to be a federal agent," he said, still holding the badge, said it like a kid with dreams of being a fireman or airline pilot. "Get out there and do what you do."

"Do you know what I do?" I asked, having some fun with him.

He screwed up his face. "Not really. But it's gotta be a damn sight better than what I'm doing."

I had to agree with that. There was no job in the prison system that appealed to me, not even the warden's. "Well, if you're serious, go online and check out the job qualifications. That would be a start. Now, if you don't mind, I'd like to go on through to the warden's office."

"Oh," he said, returning my ID and badge. "That's not possible. We're in lockdown. Will be for the rest of the day. No visitors."

"Not even to see the warden?"

"Nope," he said frowning. "Not even him."

"What's going on?" I asked.

"Nothing special. Just keeping the inmates on their toes. The warden can do one anytime. You happened to catch it."

"Means I'll have to stay around another day."

"In that case, you might want to head down to Durham. Lots to see and do there."

I returned to my car and retrieved my cell phone. "Hi. I miss you," I told Sarah when she answered. "Wanna go see Durham?"

"I miss you, too. But I have to be at Butner at two-thirty, when visiting hours begin."

"No you don't. They're in lockdown. No visitors today."

"You sure?"

"I'm standing in the parking lot. They're in lockdown till tomorrow." When she hesitated, I said, what else you got planned?" And when she didn't respond. "You still there?"

"Just thinking." A moment later she said, "Okay."

"Then it's a date?"

"Sure," she replied, and said to meet her in the lobby in thirty minutes.

I was checking the rack of tourist pamphlets when she stepped off the elevator. Like Pergamon, I watched heads turn as she crossed the lobby. She looked terrific — tailored slacks accentuating her firm rear, silk blouse, a cardigan over her shoulders, and hair in a ponytail. She strode over, took my arm and kissed me. "Hi, handsome," she said with a warm smile.

"I'll have to send the warden a thank you note," I said as we stepped outside. Once in the car, I handed her the brochures I'd selected. "Pick a place."

She fanned them out. "Such a beautiful day. We should spend it outside. How about this?" she said, holding one up.

I looked over. "The botanical garden?"

"The *Sarah* P. Duke Botanical Garden."

"Good choice," I said as we took the turn onto I-85 South.

We arrived in less than twenty minutes, parked and entered the garden via the visitors' center. "Says here, there are five miles of pathways and walks," I said, reading the brochure. "We might not find our way out."

She looked over with those molten-chocolate eyes. "Might be fun."

The brochure was right, it was an idyllic setting. There were sculpted terraces, pergolas, bridges over serene ponds, and pagodas and gazebos tucked away in private nooks where we paused in the shadows and kissed like teenagers.

As the afternoon wore on I imagined us strolling the

Mall in Washington or Alexandria's Old Town together. Midway across a Japanese bridge, I took out two coins and handed one to Sarah. "Make a wish."

She held my gaze for a moment before closing her eyes and tossing it into the pond below. "Your turn," she said. And when I had, she said, "I'll tell you mine, if you tell me yours."

"Won't that ruin it?"

"Uh-uh," she said with a child-like grin. "Once you make a wish it's out there. Nothing you say or do can change it."

"Where'd you hear that?"

"It's common knowledge."

"I never heard it."

"Well, that's because you don't travel in the right circles. You need to get out more."

I thought of my limited circle of friends and acquaintances—Theo, the other agents, and my ailing sister and her caregivers—and concluded she might be right. "It's lucky I found you."

"Lucky for me, too. Now what did you wish?"

I smiled. "All right. I wished we could sit down. My feet are killing me."

"I don't believe you."

"Why would I lie?"

"All men lie."

"What was yours?" I asked, deflecting the comment.

"I'm not telling."

"But we agreed."

"I wished we had more time together."

"That was mine, too."

"Another lie."

"I can see I'm not going to win this," I said, and we moved on.

Later, when I asked an attendant in the gift shop for

a recommendation for dinner, she said, "I think you'd enjoy Vin Rouge."

She was right. The intimate bistro, with its red walls adorned with black and white photos of French actors and starlets, was exactly what I would have selected. They offered us the option of dining al fresco in the garden or indoors, and we chose an inside table, one off in the corner. The wine and meal were perfect, and by the end of the evening we were holding hands across the table and sharing stories about ourselves.

I learned her last name was Grayson and that she'd been married before, a marriage that ended after five months when her husband was killed in a skiing accident in Canada. As a result, she moved in with her sister in New York City, which, in turn, led to a modeling stint for porno magazines.

"It isn't something I'm proud of" she explained, "but it paid well and I needed the money." She said she later hooked up with a talent agent whose main talent turned out to be pimping. Before I might say something, she squared her shoulders and said, "I wasn't a prostitute. It could've gone that way if I'd let it, but I didn't. I was a paid escort. That's as far as it went. I never went to bed with my dates, much as I knew they wanted to. The arrangement was spelled out and it was ironclad. If they wanted someone on their arm for an evening, I was available. That's all," she assured me, and I believed her. Or, at least, I wanted to believe her.

"Is Grayson your brother's name?" I asked, attempting to learn something about the man inside Butner.

She shook her head and told me Grayson is her husband's name.

"So you didn't remarry?"

"No."

"What's he in for? Your brother?"

"It's complicated," she said. "What about you? Ever been married?"

I shook my head. "Came close once, a while ago, but..."

"But what?"

"It fizzled."

"Is there a woman now?"

"No, no one."

She raised an eyebrow. "How's that possible?"

"Well, there was someone more recently, but it didn't work out either," I said of the Navy captain I met during a previous case. Carol Rutter was her name, and her one love was the Navy; at least that's how she explained it at the time. So I wasn't surprised when I saw her name on the admiral promotion list. Looking for an opportunity to re-connect, I had sent a congratulatory note, but it went unanswered.

"Another fizzle?" she said.

"It never got that far."

She nodded. "A one-sided affair."

"That's a fair description."

"No others?" she asked.

We were into our second bottle of wine when I took a long swallow and said, "You're going to think me a loser. There was one right after college, but that was another bust," I said, wondering if perhaps I wasn't opening up too much.

She reached over, squeezed my hand. "Their loss, my gain."

On balance, it turned out to be a strange night. The sex was wonderful. But I wasn't prepared for her tutorial afterward, when she loaded a small glass pipe with a nickel-sized bud of marijuana.

"This looks clean," she said with a clinical eye while holding it to the light. "Smells good, too. Has a faint peppery, lemony sweetness. I hate it when it tastes like fertilizer and chemicals. Totally destroys the experience."

Never having indulged, I watched without comment as she lit her pipe and inhaled. My refusal when she offered me a hit seemed not to bother her.

"This batch is called Jimmy Crack Corn," she said extending the baggie for my inspection. "Can you hear it snap, crackle and pop? It delivers a slow high. Not like some others that hit you like a jack hammer between the temples. This one builds up slow and lets you down easy. Later, I'll be famished. Now, I just want to cuddle and feel you inside me."

The following morning, while driving to the prison, I replayed all that happened the previous day and decided, despite her occasional marijuana sessions—which is how she described them—she was my type of woman. As for her incarcerated brother? I reasoned every family has a delinquent. Hell, my sister was no angel.

THIRTEEN

Welcome to Butner," the warden said, offering a firm handshake, while motioning me to a chair beside his desk. "I'm told you're going to help us keep Leo Kleinman alive long enough to pack him off to Israel."

Judging from his brushed military crew cut, pressed gray suit, spit-polished shoes, crisp white shirt and somber tie, and the austerity of his squared-away office, he was a no-nonsense administrator, no doubt someone who had worked his way up the Bureau of Prisons and understood the system inside and out.

"You really believe that's going to happen?" I asked. "Sending him to Israel, I mean."

He shrugged. "When it comes to politics I'll believe anything."

"What I don't understand," I said, "is why not segregate him from the rest of the inmates? I understand he doesn't want it, but why not do it anyway? It'd make everyone's job easier. It certainly would mine."

"You mean solitary," he said.

"Yeah. I understand you call it the SHU."

"Can't do it," he said, shaking his head. "He's a model prisoner. I'd have the ACLU, Amnesty International and every Zionist organization at the front gate clamoring for my scalp."

"Even if the threat is imminent?"

"We don't know that for sure."

"Then why am I here?"

"You'll find the answer to that question about two hundred miles north of here, in Washington. But you already know that. Concerning the threat, I didn't say it isn't real. Someone on the outside wants him dead," he said. "And he's pretty clever the way he's going about it."

"You mean getting someone inside riled up enough to do it?"

"Exactly. Tongues wag in here, and it doesn't take much to turn on some knucklehead."

"We're leaning toward a woman as the writer," I told him.

"A woman? You sure?"

"According to the psycholinguistic folks on the FBI's Behavioral Science team, the writer's female."

"Interesting. What else?"

"We have to consider she might be employed here at Butner."

He looked doubtful. "That seems like a stretch."

"Perhaps. But without much to go on we have to examine all possibilities. As you indicated, those letters are intended to incite, suggesting she may know the system."

"So you'll want a list of our female employees?"

I nodded. "Any problem with that?"

He considered the question. "No. I'll email it to you by close of business today."

"What are the odds? Of an inmate killing him?"

"Like I said, there's no shortage of knuckleheads in here. Plus, you have to consider who he is."

"A traitor?"

"A traitor and a Jew."

"What's being Jewish got to do with it?"

"You don't know much about prison life, do you?"

"My job's putting 'em in here. After that, I figure, they're your problem."

"They sure are," he said with a sigh. "And the problems never end."

"I didn't mean to sound flip," I said. "I apologize."

"No apology necessary. It is what it is."

"So, why's being a Jew a problem? There are plenty of Jews in prison. You must have a fair number here. They all disliked?"

"No and yes. No, we don't have many and, yes, they're all disliked."

"That true throughout the system?" I asked.

He nodded. "They don't fit in. And that's how they like it."

"Doesn't make sense. Why create problems for themselves?"

"You'd have to ask them. From where I sit, they don't mix if they can help it. Of course, they have to in work details, but that's about as far as it goes."

"I heard there's a large Jewish population in one of your upstate New York prisons."

"Otisville," he said nodding. "About seventy miles from the city. A medium-security facility and a camp. Both have a big Jewish population."

"How's that work for them?"

He laughed. "They run the place. Not literally. But they do pretty well for themselves. Not so here."

"Wonder why Kleinman wasn't sent there."

His expression hardened. "Don't think his legal team didn't try."

"What happened?"

"Didn't you study the case?"

"Not the whole case. Haven't had time."

"Secretary of Defense Weinberger wanted to hang him. Others pushed for the maximum facility in Florence, Colorado. Where he'd rot in solitary."

"And?"

He shook his head. "Too many powerful connections."

"Like the Israelis?"

He shrugged. "Israelis. Americans. So he wound up here."

"A compromise."

He nodded. "But only if he behaves. He screws up and it's the first flight to Florence. He knows it, and has been smart enough to keep his nose clean."

"How's he get along with the other inmates?"

"Pretty much keeps to himself. You got a minute?" he asked, glancing at his watch, which I took to mean that was about all the time I had left with him. When I nodded, he said, "He doesn't have much choice. Except for the Jews, no one wants anything to do with him.

"It's how the system works. Prejudices get magnified in here. With time on their hands, inmates can make mountains out of mole hills. So when they see a group with extra privileges, like the Jews, it fuels resentment."

"What kind of privileges?"

"More holidays. And kosher meals."

"What's so special about kosher meals?"

"Higher quality food, which they trade for favors."

"I hadn't thought about that."

"Why would you? Those kosher meals are like currency. There's also home leave during high holy days, a privilege not accorded gentiles."

"That can't apply to Kleinman," I said.

He waved his hand. "Of course not. We'd never let him out. But enough of the others get to go. Then there's the ones who get their sentences commuted."

"How's that happen?"

"Political pull. It doesn't happen often, but it happens."

"So," I asked, sensing my time was about up, "what's to be done about protecting Kleinman?"

"Like I said, not a helluva lot. We'll continue lockdowns and shakedowns, and relying on informants. If we're lucky, we'll learn something that enables us to prevent an attack."

"I wouldn't want your job."

He forced a laugh. "There are days I wouldn't, either. So, you ready to meet the infamous traitor?"

"Ready as ever."

"Watch him. He's a sly devil," he cautioned, before picking up the phone and instructing Kleinman's unit team manager to deliver him to the Attorney Visiting Room, adjacent to the Visitors Room. "He'll play you like a piano."

"I was thinking it would be better to meet away from the other inmates, somewhere private, like a conference room."

He shook his head. "Uh-uh. This has to look like he's meeting his attorney. Anywhere else, and they'll assume he's ratting someone out. We don't want that, and neither does he."

I followed a guard to the admin building and a small windowless room with a gray metal table anchored to the floor and two sturdy plastic chairs. Kleinman pushed his bulk from the table and rose as I entered. I noticed his uniform was freshly pressed and thought he needn't have bothered. He wasn't going to win points for neatness from me.

"We finally meet," he said, extending a plump hand, which I ignored. "I've heard a lot about you. All good."

"Bullshit. There's no one here who knows me. And if

there is, he wouldn't be singing my praises."

"Not inside," he said with a grin I found annoying. "Outside. From a mutual acquaintance."

"We don't have any mutual acquaintances," I assured him.

The grin widened, showing a row of stained teeth. "Someone you recently had dinner with." Noting my confusion, he added, "Max Goodman."

I didn't like him playing me, and I said, "Let's get something straight, Kleinman. I don't care what you heard, or who it came from. As far as I'm concerned, you committed treason and should've been executed. But you weren't, and now I have to save your sorry ass. And if I fail... well… I don't imagine I'd lose much sleep over it. We clear on that?"

"Very clear," he said, losing the grin and running his fingers through his gray beard.

"Good. Now, what can you tell me that'll help us find the letter writer? You must receive plenty of threatening letters. How do these differ from the others?"

"There's nothing to compare. I don't get hate letters."

"I don't believe you," I said.

"I mean, except for these anonymous ones. I used to get a shit-load in the beginning. Crackpots spewing anti-Semitic venom but, unlike this loon, they rarely sent more than one. This guy's on a mission, and won't be satisfied till I'm dead or maimed."

"And you think they'll incite someone?"

He adjusted his wire rimmed glasses, while rubbing the bridge of his nose. "Absolutely."

"Have you been threatened?"

"Not directly. But I'm sensing hostility." I laughed and he snapped, "What's so funny?"

"Come on, Kleinman. You're living in a hostile environment. This isn't kindergarten. I've seen the inmate rule book. It's gotta be an inch thick. Do this. Don't do that. Sit here. Don't sit. Don't mouth-off. You can't get a roll of toilet paper without someone's permission. This place breeds hostility."

"So, you're an expert on prison life."

"I didn't say that."

"Then don't tell me what it's like inside. I've been at it going on thirty years."

"Okay," I said, but he wasn't about to let it go.

"You don't survive in here by not knowing what's happening around you. A blade of grass out there on the field grows in the wrong direction, I know it," he said thumping his chest. "I can tell you every inmate's hot button. And every correction officer's, too."

"I get it," I said.

"I don't think you do," he said, his anger growing. "One glance down the chow line and I know whether a guy's wife or girlfriend visited him that day, or didn't visit him. I look in a man's eyes, I know what he's thinking."

"Point taken."

"The point, Agent Shore, is when I say I'm sensing hostility it isn't a figment of my imagination. Something's changed. Men who were friendly or acknowledged me, shun me now. I'm getting looks I didn't get before. What else is it, if it isn't those damn letters? Here," he said removing one from his pocket and tossing it across the table. "Got this yesterday."

> *Dear Leo,*
>
> *You'll be getting yours soon!!! The men inside know about your deal with Israel, the country that tried sinking an unarmed U.S. Navy ship, and killed and wounded two-thirds of the crew. They also know about the deposits to your Israeli bank account and your Israeli passport and your pending release. They*

don't like it, Leo!!! They don't like the idea of a traitor going free one bit!!! You're going to get what's coming to you, you miserable traitor!!! Keep alert. Your days are numbered!!!

"Interesting," I said. "It reads like the writer's got a handle on what's happening inside."

"Yeah. Like he's looking over my shoulder," he said with a shudder. "It's creepy."

"Since you know so much about this place, is there anyone inside with a connection to the *Liberty*? A crewman's relative? A shipmate? Anyone? You must've done some digging."

He looked at me as if I were an idiot. "Of course I did. I've studied everything I get my hands on about that damn ship. Compared every crewman's name, dead and alive with the inmate list."

"And?"

"And nothing. No matches. No connections. What about you? Those letters are coming from outside. What're you learning?"

"We have a few leads," I said.

"Like?"

"We're pretty certain the writer's a woman."

He raised his eyebrows. "No shit? A woman?"

He asked how I knew, and I explained about forensic psycholinguistics and what we detected from the writer's style and content.

"Is that it?"

"That's all I'm prepared to discuss. Could there be more to this than a connection to the *Liberty*? Is there something you're not telling us?"

"Like what? The letters, they all reference the attack on the ship. What else is there?"

"It's possible this *Liberty* thing is a ruse," I said.

"I don't follow you," he said.

"Well, I understand Jewish inmates aren't well liked, especially among the blacks. That you enjoy privileges others don't. That some Jews with connections have had their sentences reduced or commuted."

"If that's true, why me and not the others?"

"You're also a traitor."

"I'm not a traitor! What I did, I did for an ally."

"Yeah. I read all about it. As to why you, how about the influential people intervening on your behalf and the organizations pressing for your release? You don't think that fosters resentment?"

He laughed. "And you see where that got me."

"Still. You don't think that might piss off some people?"

He stared at me for a long moment. "If you knew anything about my case, you'd know I was eligible for parole after serving eight years and six months, and I never once went before the board to ask for a hearing."

"That's because you know they'd never grant it."

He squared his round shoulders. "It's because a parole implies guilt, and I'm innocent."

I laughed. "Get serious."

"You been to Dachau?"

"No."

"Well, I have. When I was a teenager. It was fucking horrible. I also went to school in Israel one summer. I've been to the Syrian border, the Egyptian border, and the Jordanian border. I looked across and saw the cold hard faces of the enemy. What I did, I did for an ally. An ally surrounded by enemies."

"I'm not buying it."

"They're an *ally*," he repeated, his voice rising. "And they weren't getting the assistance they needed."

"So *you* decided to pass along sensitive compartmented information without concern for *our* national security?"

This wasn't how the interview was supposed to go, but I couldn't let the weasel get away with this absurdity.

"They're our only ally in that whole turbulent region. Who else was going to help them?"

"I see. And I suppose South Africa was an ally entitled to our military secrets? And Indonesia? And Colombia? You went to them before finding a willing buyer in Israel," I reminded him.

"What's the use," he said shaking his head.

"My sentiments, exactly. So spare me the bullshit and let's get down to who wants you dead."

"If I knew, I'd tell you. Which is why we have to work together."

"Which is why I'm here," I said.

"Well, what else have you uncovered other than the writer's a female?"

"Not much. It's old-fashioned police work. Focusing on immediate and extended family members of the ship's crew. With luck, we'll find her before her letters incite someone. Meanwhile, you could help yourself by going into the Special Housing Unit."

He laughed. "You joking?" And when he saw I wasn't, he folded his arms and said, "Sure would make your job easier, me going in the SHU."

"It won't be for the first time. Your record indicates you sought protection at Petersburg, again at Springfield, Mississippi, and in Marion, Illinois."

"Check the dates," he said. "Things were different then. I was new in the system, and guys were trying to make a name for themselves. Happens often with a high-profile prisoner. Even Bernie Madoff had problems when he got here. But eventually things calm down and life goes on."

"Were things calm here at Butner when you went into the SHU? That was several years after you were in the system."

"That was also right after the World Trade Center got hit, when there were rumors Israel had something to do with it. I haven't had any problems since. Not till these cockamamie letters started arriving. And I'm damned if I'll let some fruitcake push me into solitary."

"Not even till we get a handle on her?"

"She'd be delighted to have me locked away if she can't have me killed. No contact with anyone, not even my wife. Well, I've had my share of solitary, and it's no picnic."

Moving on, I asked, "Has this person contacted your wife or other family members?"

I could tell the question bothered him.

"Just me. You read the letters. The woman wants someone inside to kill me. What good does contacting them do?"

"Do they know about the letters?"

"Only my wife. I haven't told my parents or my sister. They have enough to worry about."

"Would they tell you if they got any communication from this person, say a phone call or email?"

He was tapping his foot anxiously. "Damn it! They aren't the target, I am. And that's the way I want it."

"I'm sure you've already thought about this, but they may also be a target. If those letters don't do what the writer wants, she may go after your wife or…"

"Shut up! I don't want to hear that!" he said shaking his head.

We sat in silence until he settled down. "I understand it isn't a pleasant thought," I said, "but it's something to consider. Now, are they being threatened or harassed, too? Any of them?"

"Uh-uh. Just me."

"Would they tell you if they were?"

"In the beginning, after I was sentenced, they told me when they were contacted. Hollow threats that never amounted to anything."

"What about now?"

"There's no reason to believe they wouldn't tell me." He was tugging his beard, his leg beginning to bounce. Then, leaning forward, he implored, "Leave my parents out of this. They're old and frail and don't need you knocking on the door telling them I'm in danger. If I thought they were at risk or could help, I'd tell you. So, please stay away from them."

"Does that go for your wife, as well?" The question made him stiffen.

"What do you mean?"

"If the writer did reach her, would she tell you?"

"Immediately. She wouldn't sit on something like this."

"Any objections to contacting her?"

He shook his head. "Next time she visits I'll tell her to call you."

"And when might that be?"

He licked his full lips. "Today. I'll talk to her."

I nodded. "Good. I'm staying at the Inn at Creedmoor. She can reach me there. Now what about your first wife, Priscilla? She's out now. Have you heard from her?"

He flinched at the mention of her name and for a moment his gaze drifted into the distance. "Poor, Priscilla," he muttered. "She didn't deserve prison."

Didn't deserve prison? That wasn't how I read it. In reviewing the case, I noted she pled guilty to receiving stolen government property and accessory after the fact to possession of national defense documents. For that, she served three years and four months before being paroled back in 1990. The record on her involvement was well documented. She and Kleinman enjoyed first-class trips abroad, and shopping sprees to high-end stores and boutiques. But I didn't contradict him on it. There seemed little to be gained challenging him on that point.

"Priscilla returned to Vogel, her maiden name, after her release," he said. "I doubt this *meshugana* woman would know how to contact her. What about you? Are you married?"

I don't share personal information with criminals, but he caught me by surprise and I answered without thinking. "No. Not yet."

"Not yet, eh? What are you waiting for? You got a woman?" he asked with a crooked grin. When I didn't respond, he said, "Hmm. You aren't a *fagilah*?"

"Excuse me?"

"A *fagilah*. Someone who likes men."

"What about the envelopes?" I asked. "Do you have them?"

He nodded. "They come from Tennessee. All of them."

"I'd like to see them."

"Sure. If they let me give them to my wife, she can give them to you. It's up to the warden."

"I'll speak to him about it," I said. "And this letter, mind if I hold onto it?"

"May as well. It isn't doing me any good."

I picked up the letter and placed it in my leather case. "Unless you have something more to share with me, I think we're done for now."

"Too bad," he said with a mischievous tone. "I was starting to enjoy your company."

As I stood to leave, I said, "Anybody asks, I'm your attorney. We don't want someone thinking you're a snitch."

He stood and adjusted his yarmulke. "I know the

game." Then, with a smirk, he added, "Know it better than you."

Before driving away from Butner, I re-read the letter Kleinman had given me. How, I wondered, could she be certain the inmates knew of his Israeli connections? The list of employees would be worth looking at.

FOURTEEN

Chatham had been observing Tom Kelly, the new guy, a skinny kid with stringy hair and a weak mouth, familiarizing himself with the prison system. He saw him deferring to the correction officers, asking questions of them rather than seeking advice from inmates. He watched him position himself opposite the COs in open areas, shifting to stay in their line of sight, to keep from being harassed or attacked by fellow inmates—all telltale signs of insecurity. Chatham didn't have much time, he had to reach Kelly before the COs turned him into a snitch, which was when they recruited new guys, when they were most vulnerable.

Deciding it was time to move, Chatham found him on the walking track one afternoon before the four o'clock head count. Typical of rookie prisoners, Kelly was trying to be invisible, keeping his head down, hunching his shoulders and swinging his arms tightly beside him. He was also steering clear of other inmates on the track, especially blacks, slowing his pace to avoid overtaking them, or falling back when they were about to overtake him. And though no one appeared to be aware of or interested in him, Chatham knew they too were taking his measure.

"How's it going?" Chatham asked, coming up behind him.

The kid—he looked about nineteen or so—nearly jumped out of his uniform. Snapping his head around, he jerked his fists up and stepped back, looking around to see who else had snuck up on him. But there was only Chatham, all six-foot-six inches of muscle gazing down at him without a trace of hostility. Kelly lowered his hands, but not before taking another step back. "Didn't see you."

"I seen you around," Chatham said, lapsing into his good-ole-boy manner. And when Kelly didn't respond, he asked again, "How's it going?"

Lost in the taller man's shadow, Kelly squinted into the afternoon sun. "You gotta be kidding. It sucks."

Chatham nodded. "Holding area usually does. What's it been, about three weeks they got you bunked in with those spooks?"

"Going on four," Kelly freely admitted.

"Ain't no fun, I'll bet. You being the only white man," he said, as they resumed walking at a slower pace than Kelly had been walking.

Kelly snorted. "That's an understatement."

"First time inside?" And when Kelly nodded, he asked, "How old are you?"

"Twenty-three. Well, almost. Six weeks shy."

"I figured you for younger."

"Happens a lot," Kelly said.

"What do you go by?"

"Whaddya mean?" Kelly said.

"Your name."

"Kelly. Tom Kelly."

"That's it?"

"What else?"

"Folks inside tend to go by a nickname."

"Don't got one," Kelly said. "What's yours?"

"Professor. Some folks call me Professor."

"You a teacher?"

Chatham smiled. "Because of my college degrees."

"Pleased to me you, Professor," he said, extending his hand.

"Real name's Chatham. Lew Chatham. I answer to both," he said, clasping the younger man's hand. "Where's home?"

"South Jersey." And when Chatham didn't respond, he said, "Toms River?"

"Yeah, I heard of it. Near Atlantic City."

"'Bout fifty miles north of A.C."

"What're you in for?"

"Larceny theft," Kelly said. "How about you?"

"How'd they nail you?" Chatham said, ignoring the question.

"Selling government property to a federal agent."

Chatham laughed. "That'll do it."

"Shoulda known better," Kelly said, opening up. "I had a smooth operation going at Lakehurst."

"The naval air station?"

Kelly nodded. "Unloading parts and equipment to a coupla mooks from A.C. They'd give me a shopping list and I'd pull the stuff from the surplus warehouse where I worked and move it off base. No problems."

"Then you got greedy," Chatham said.

Kelly turned and looked up at him. "How'd you know?"

"Lucky guess. So what happened?"

"Like I said, everything was fine. Then I hear this new guy wants in. When I told them I don't do business with people I don't know, they said not to worry. Said they knew him from A. C. That he was connected. A standup guy who'll buy anything. So I figure as long as they're vouching for him it's okay, and we start doing business. Him and me. Soon, he's got me hauling all kinds of shit out of there, and I'm making good money."

Chatham shook his head. "Set you up."

"Exactly. He was a fed, and the rat bastards who introduced him testified against me. A sweet deal for them and… Well, here I am. It was dumb."

"It was dumb for a lot of reasons. Your first offense?"

He nodded. "Earned me thirty-six months."

"We all make mistakes, or we wouldn't be here. The important thing is you learn from them, so you don't get nabbed the next time."

Kelly let out a short laugh. "I'm learning all right. I learned not to do business with the feds. I also learned about con air."

Chatham grinned. "You're getting a helluva education."

"Fucking marshals. Shuffled me halfway around the country for three miserable weeks before delivering me here. I must've seen the inside of a dozen rat-infested jails. Three weeks of hell. I coulda walked here from Philly faster."

"It's part of the harassment. Next time, if they don't remand you, have your lawyer or a friend deliver you on the date the court gives you. You walk right in with your papers and say, 'Here I am.' You never want to put yourself in the marshals' hands. They'll jerk you around every time."

"I wish I'd known that before. Lousy public defender never said anything."

"Well, you're here now."

"Yeah, I'm here. Stuck in that fucking holding area."

"Those niggers giving you shit?" Chatham asked as they were overtaking two black inmates.

"Jesus!" Kelly whispered, averting the hard stares

aimed at them.

"Don't worry," Chatham assured him. "You're in good company."

Unconvinced, Kelly hastened his pace, then fell back again when Chatham failed to join him.

Chatham repeated, "They giving you shit?"

"Every fucking day," he said keeping his voice low. "I ain't had a decent night's sleep, what with the yelling. It's a goddamn zoo in there. And it smells like one, too."

"They laying hands on you?"

"Naw. None of that. Just hassling me. Letting me know who's boss. Setting down rules. First time I sat on a guy's bunk I thought he was going to kill me."

"That's not a nigger rule. You never sit on a guy's rack lest he's there and he says it's okay. Don't let your sheet touch his rack either. And never touch another guy's stuff. These rules apply across the board. Remember that."

"I will."

"And another thing. Don't reach across the table and don't touch another man's food. You do, and you'll get your fingers broke, or worse."

Kelly was nodding at each bit of advice, paying little attention to their surroundings, when Chatham suddenly stopped at the edge of the track. Shifting his attention to a group of blacks lounging around a nearby picnic table, Chatham said in a clear, loud voice, "And don't let any nigger tell you who's boss."

Kelly saw their heads snap up and suddenly the air was charged. Standing stone-still and slack-jawed, his mouth going dry, he struggled with what to do next while scanning the yard for a CO who would disperse the fight when it erupted and before he got his skull cracked. But there was no one; only a few inmates playing horseshoes out of earshot. And while no one spoke, there was no mistaking the hostility of the four blacks, as they rose as one, folding their arms across their broad chests. Should he continue walking, leaving Chatham to fight his own battle, or stay with him and take his lumps?

Sweat trickled down Kelly's back as he considered his options. The blacks weren't looking at him. Their eyes were fixed on Chatham, whose warrior pose equaled theirs. After an eternity of seconds in which no one crossed the fifteen-foot-or-so strip of grass separating them, and it was apparent no one would, Chatham turned and nudged Kelly in the direction in which they'd been walking.

It wasn't till they were at what Kelly determined was a safe distance, that he cleared his throat and said, "That was hairy." And when Chatham laughed, he said, "What? You don't think so?"

"I'll tell you what I think," Chatham said. "I think you worry too much."

"You blame me? I'm squeezed in with twenty blacks, and there's only one of me."

"Still. You stuck by me, and I appreciate that," Chatham declared. "Tomorrow, we'll have you out of there and in a white neighborhood by noon."

"We?"

"The Brotherhood. The Aryan Brotherhood."

"You can do that? Get me moved?"

Chatham nodded. "We don't walk away from a friend."

* * *

Rasheed stepped from the shower stall, a rock in one hand, the glass shards he'd just ground into slivers wrapped in a dishrag in the other. It was mid-day and he was alone in the bloc, the other inmates still at work. Only the kitchen staff, with their oddball work schedule, were free to access the showers at this hour. Gathering his clothes from the bench, he dressed and shoved the objects in his pockets. He would toss the stone in the bushes before reaching the mess hall.

Inside, the kosher meals delivered that morning were stacked beside the steam table. While serving lunch earlier, Rasheed had noticed mashed yams were part of the evening kosher meal, which is when he decided to introduce the ground glass. He'd been observing Kleinman closely at every meal, and was pleased to see him ingesting food like a human vacuum, barely pausing between bites to stuff another forkful in his face. Rasheed felt confident he'd swallow the entire serving without detecting the glass.

You gonna die tonight, Jew boy, he thought fingering the washcloth in his pocket. *And ain't nobody's gonna know who done it.*

"Hey, Roberts," the correction officer called, causing Rasheed to wince.

He hated the sound of his former name. *It's Rasheed, asshole*, he wanted to tell the dumb CO. *Jamal Rasheed.* Instead, he turned and said, "Yes, sir?"

"You got scullery duty," the CO informed him with a nod toward the tiled sink area behind the serving line.

"No, sir. I'm serving."

"Not tonight. Watkins is sick. Now move it."

Rasheed gritted his teeth as his gaze drifted to the kosher meals. *Get you another day, motherfucker.*

FIFTEEN

We planned to meet in the lobby at six after Sarah returned from Butner, then head across the street to Pergamon for drinks and dinner. With time to spare, I checked in with Theo at headquarters.

"I met with Kleinman today," I told him, "but didn't learn much. He agreed to hand over the envelopes. I'm hoping they'll provide something more than we gleaned from the letters. Any luck tracking down the *Liberty* crew members?"

"Still working it. Nothing to report yet."

"There's something else," I said, and told him what the warden had said about the writer sounding like she knew what was happening inside. "Her latest letter has me thinking she may even work at the prison. The warden's providing a list of female employees. I'll forward it to you. If we're lucky there'll be a connection with the ship."

"Speaking of letters," Theo said, "our friends at the Bureau did a statistical analysis and found a pattern in the writer's word choices and groups of phrases."

"How's that help us?" I asked.

"It won't help narrow the search or ID her but it provides a unique profile of the woman."

"And?"

"Without getting technical, these choices aren't made consciously."

"Meaning?" On occasion Theo's genius needs prodding. This was one of them.

"It'll confirm she's the writer, when we do ID her."

"Like matching her prints or DNA," I said.

"Exactly. It can be used in court."

"Sorta putting the cart before the horse."

"You don't sound very enthusiastic," he replied.

"Well, frankly, I'm not. I'm no closer to finding her than I was before hauling myself down here."

Always the optimist, Theo offered the usual bromide about good police work being ninety percent footwork and ten percent luck. "Cheer up. You've tracked down perps with fewer leads. You'll nab this one."

When the warden's email arrived listing the female employees—seventeen full-timers and six part-timers—I forwarded it to Theo as promised. Next, I alerted the front desk I was expecting a package and to call when it arrived. With little else to do, I stretched out and closed my eyes.

An hour later, the phone rang. "Your package arrived, Mr. Shore," the receptionist announced.

I rubbed the sleep from my eyes, laced up my shoes, and headed for the lobby expecting to find Kleinman's wife there. The elevator doors opened and there was Sarah looking splendid.

"Where're you going? I thought we had a date," she said, stepping out, the doors shutting behind her.

"We do. Just picking up something at the front desk. See you at six."

I was too late. She was gone. The large brown Butner Prison envelope she left was addressed to *NCIS Agent Jerzy Shore, c/o Creedmoor Inn*. It held about a dozen self-sealing envelopes, which meant no saliva and no DNA. Clever woman. As expected, neither was there a return address, but there was one helpful lead. All but one were postmarked with various 372 zip codes, which the Postal Service website listed as the Nashville area. The exception was the 37024 zip code in the nearby town of Brentwood, just south of Nashville. And, since both towns were over five hundred miles from Butner, I had to assume the woman wasn't a prison employee.

When I phoned Theo his first comment was, "I'm fast, but not that fast."

"Whatya mean?"

"Got your email, but I haven't done anything with it yet."

"It appears she isn't an employee," I said, before sharing this latest info on the zip codes. "Could mean she lives in Brentwood and mails her letters in Nashville. Got lazy one day, and posted that one in her home town."

"Or, she just might pass through those sites and doesn't live near any of them," Theo volunteered.

"Well, we've got to start somewhere," I said.

"I'll do some digging on this end. See if there are any crewmembers living in the area," he said.

"Tell me about it when I get back."

"Better hurry. Chief's been asking after you."

I groaned. One of the more pleasant aspects of working cold cases was the independence that came with the job. I could proceed at my own pace and without outside interference. However, it wasn't working that way lately. The chief began giving me rudder orders in the decades-old death case of the Naval Academy midshipman, and now he was doing it again. "I wish he'd stop meddling," I said.

"Cut him some slack," Theo countered. "These high

profile cases come with a lot of top-down pressure." I reluctantly agreed, and he said, "So, if he asks, what'll I tell him?"

I thought of Sarah. We hadn't talked about what would happen after we headed north. "Tell him he'll see me tomorrow."

Returning to my room, I swapped my shirt and tie for a Polo shirt and blazer, splashed on some cologne, and headed for the lobby. I was waiting by the front desk when Sarah stepped off the elevator, and I had to laugh when a guy at the coffee bar splashed his companion's drink while elbowing him.

She kissed my cheek and said, "Happy to see me?"

"Always," I replied, steering her past the two oglers.

"Let's go back to Vin Rouge in Durham," she said when we reached the parking lot. "It's much nicer than Pergamon."

Neither of us spoke much on the ride down. I'd been mulling over the postmarks on the envelopes, and I figured Sarah probably was thinking about her brother, whom she had just left.

"Did you accomplish what you intended at Butner?" she asked after we were seated at the same distant table.

"It wasn't as productive as I'd hoped."

"What were you expecting?" When I hesitated, she said, "You don't have to talk about it if it's against the rules."

I shook my head. "There are no rules. It's just... I don't usually discuss my cases."

"I understand," she said.

I shrugged. "I suppose it doesn't matter. It's not my usual type of case, preventing a crime rather than trying to solve one."

"Is that making this one more difficult?"

I thought about that. "Not difficult so much as

different." I explained how criminals typically leave clues at crime scenes, and lacking a crime scene was hampering me. She looked confused, and I said, "An inmate's being threatened, and I thought he might provide something that could lead me to the source of the threat."

"And he didn't? Provide anything useful?"

"It's too early to say. I got a couple of leads, which brings me to us."

"*Us?*" she said, her eyes widening.

I laughed. "I don't mean you have anything to do with the case. What I'm trying to say—clearly, not very well—is I'm returning to Quantico tomorrow, and was wondering… That is, once we're back home… You in Bethesda, me in Arlington… Well… We might continue seeing each other."

I watched her gaze drop to her hands, and gauged her silence to mean I had miscalculated. That what happened between us was all that would happen between us.

"Jerzey, what we did—what I did, going to bed with you—wasn't done lightly."

I tried assuring her I didn't think it was, but she held up her hand. "Please. I don't want you thinking it was the booze, or that I fall into bed with whoever comes along."

"I wasn't thinking that at all," I said.

Ignoring my protest, she said, "It was neither. Rather, I was drawn to you. I felt it the moment you came to my defense at Pergamon. Call it chemistry, magic. I don't know. But it happened, and I'm glad of it."

"So, no regrets?"

She shook her head. "Certainly not."

"That's a relief," I said, thinking how I'd misread signals in previous relationships.

"Why would you think that?"

"I don't know," I said, feeling foolish. "I just didn't want this to be one-sided."

She reached over and laid her hand on mine. "Silly man."

"So..., we'll be getting together after leaving here?"

"Absolutely."

SIXTEEN

Lew Chatham stepped out of the shadows. "Where you going?" he asked, startling Tom Kelly, who spun around raising his fists, then quickly dropping them. He was still carrying bruises from his last night in the holding area—along with a few new ones, delivered after word got back about the little white guy tagging along with the Aryan Brotherhood warrior on the walking track.

"Jesus, Lew, you can't keep coming up on me like that."

"You heading in there?" Chatham said, nodding toward the weight room.

"Yeah. Do some reps."

"You don't want to go now."

"Why not?" Kelly said, creasing his brow.

"It's their time. You go in and you'll get more of what they gave you back in the holding area."

Kelly peered inside while rubbing a recently inflicted purple knob on his scalp, then stepped away. Stealing a second look, he said, "Shit. So when do I use it?"

"Come back later, when it's our time. And when the stink is out of there."

"What happens then?"

"What happens is the place belongs to us, just like they own it now."

"I'm never gonna make it in here. Too many goddamn unwritten rules."

Chatham let the comment pass. "How's it going in the laundry?"

"Sucks," he said of the job assigned him a week ago.

"What's wrong?"

"More of the same. Head guy's black. Gives me all the shit details."

"Figures," Chatham said nodding. "There's an opening over in the warehouse."

"No kidding!" Kelly said, perking up.

"It could be yours."

"Really? What do I hafta do to get it?"

"Got a problem working with Albanians?"

"Shit. I'll work with anybody to get outta there. Don't matter they're from Alabama, so long's they ain't black. Fuckers gave me these," he said, lifting his shirt to reveal a row of bruises down his back. "I don't shape up, they said, they're gonna throw me in the fuckin' dryer."

"Albanians are from Albania," Chatham explained.

Kelly shrugged. "Never heard of it."

"It's a country in southern Europe. And they're white."

"They speak American, don't they?"

"Yeah. They speak American."

"Then it's all good," he said clapping his hands. "I can handle the rest. That's what I was doing at Lakehurst. Working the warehouse."

"I remember. Which is why I figured you for it. It's a creampuff job. The guys only hustle when they deliver supplies. Rest of the time, they sit around and fill orders." Pausing, he cautioned, "One thing. Albanians are a tough breed. You don't cross them."

"No problemo. You can arrange it?"

"I'll let you know."

"That'd be swell." Then squinting, he said, "So, what's the catch? Gotta be a catch."

"Of course, there's always a catch. 'Nothing for nothing,' as John McCormack used to say."

"He an Aryan?"

"No," Chatham said. Then, throwing his arm around Kelly's shoulder and steering him away from the gym, he said, "He was a congressman. Speaker of the House before we were born. Whenever a new guy came around asking favors, he'd throw his arm around his shoulder, like this, and pointing to the empty space above his office door, he'd say, 'That's the motto of this office.' And when the guy gave ole John a curious look, as they always did, he'd say, 'That's right. Nothing for nothing.' Get it?"

"Yeah. Ain't that how it always is?" And when Chatham nodded, Kelly asked, "So what's it gonna cost?"

Chatham grinned. "I like a man who gets to the point. It isn't so much what it'll cost you, as what you'll get out of it."

Kelly wrinkled his brow. "Out of what? You're confusing me. Either it'll cost me or it won't."

"It's more of a *quid pro quo* arrangement," Chatham said.

"A quid what?"

"We do something for you and you do something in return."

"Yeah. Like I said. What's it gonna cost?"

"That's not how we see it. We see it as an opportunity."

"You keep saying *we*."

"The Brotherhood."

"An opportunity for the Brotherhood?"

"A mutual opportunity. You move to the warehouse and we get a new member."

Kelly stopped walking and, tilted his head sideways. "You want *me* in the Brotherhood?"

Chatham nodded. "We're always looking for standup guys."

"Me?"

"This isn't a service club. We don't let anyone in. We figure you're the right kind of guy. If you don't want in, that's okay. No harm, no foul. Do your time and move on."

"Do my time alone," Kelly said. "In the laundry, or wherever they stick me."

Chatham shrugged. "That's how it's done." And as Kelly considered his options, Chatham said, "Keep in mind, membership comes with benefits."

"I'm beginning to see that. If it wasn't for you I'd still be…"

"For the Brotherhood. If it wasn't for the Brotherhood," Chatham corrected him. "We watch over our own."

"Yeah, the Brotherhood. If it wasn't for the Brotherhood I'd be back in that godforsaken holding area sleeping with one eye open."

"And we'll move you out of the laundry, too."

"How soon?"

"Soon as you join."

"Where do I sign?"

Chatham smiled. "Not so fast, my friend. You never want to sign a contract without first reading it."

"There's a contract?"

"Not a *written* contract. A set of rules."

"What kind of rules?"

"Rules that protect us."

Kelly thought about it. "Makes sense. And then I'm a member?"

"After the initiation."

"What kind of initiation?"

"We'll talk about that later," Chatham said. "First the rules."

SEVENTEEN

Laura Greene arrived home at the usual time, exhausted from a day on her feet in the clinic and frustrated that Leo Kleinman was still alive and uninjured. Her thoughts while sorting her mail were on what more she might do to change matters. Seeing the letter from her friend made her pause, and she put it aside to be read later.

After a light supper, washed down with generous amounts of wine, she took her glass and the letter into the living room, where she propped her feet on the ottoman and tore open the envelope.

Dear Laura,

I will be brief because I don't have the energy to be otherwise. I know you'll forgive me for not telling you sooner. These past few weeks have been excruciating. You know, my father's condition has been worsening, but you don't know how bad it's gotten. What I haven't mentioned was that I was forced to seek help from the good folks at hospice. Last week, under their care and supervision, he passed away. Like your uncle, he was a fighter to the end. And while it may sound callous to one unfamiliar with our struggles, I know you understand, when I say I'm relieved. Relieved because he is at rest and his long nightmare has finally ended.

While it doesn't seem possible today, I want to think I am burying all the painful memories with him and I will have only the good ones to reflect on. To that end, I'm placing what little faith I have left in the Lord, hoping He allows me to think of my father without seeing him broken from battling years of surgeries and therapy sessions.

I could never say this to anyone but you. As terrible as it sounds, I often wished the Israelis had sunk the damn ship with all hands aboard as they intended. At least that would have ended it once and for all.

Keep me in your prayers.

Love,

Hattie

Laura closed her eyes and sank into the cushion, warm tears wetting her cheeks. Her sorrow soon turned to anger as she pondered the innocent lives damaged over the years by the attack—the spouses, children, extended families, even strangers, who suffered alongside these battle-scarred sailors when caring for them became too burdensome—as had happened with her own aunt, whose decades of alcoholism not only consumed her life, but ended that of a young motorcyclist when she swerved into oncoming traffic early one Sunday morning. Laura long ago gave up trying to guess the number of victims beyond the crew. It was difficult enough caring for her widowed uncle, who had believed in God before the attack and returned home convinced God had ceased believing in him.

She carefully folded Hattie's letter and returned it to the envelope. She would phone her when she had the strength to offer her friend positive, uplifting thoughts. For now, she could only pray she'd find the peace she sought, though Laura somehow doubted she would.

Both women were close in age. They had met years earlier at a *Liberty* reunion and forged an instant friendship that grew stronger across the miles as their lives spiraled downward. Both had quit college to tend to broken families, a burden that later contributed to two failed marriages for Laura and spinsterhood for her friend. And when Laura's uncle had finally succumbed to his injuries, Hattie had stepped forward. Now it was Laura's turn to travel to her friend's side, no matter how many Celexa she had to swallow to get there.

She wished she could tell Hattie that Kleinman had gotten what he deserved, but sadly, neither Chatham nor Rasheed had responded as Laura had hoped. They had listened to her, even appeared sympathetic, but she couldn't be sure how they felt. Whatever they were thinking, they weren't sharing it with her.

If someone didn't step forward soon she'd place Kleinman's name on the Call Out list and do the job herself.

EIGHTEEN

Jerzy asked Sarah over breakfast, what time she was heading north?

"I'm not," she replied. "I'm driving back tomorrow."

"Last night you said today."

"I decided to stay over. My brother's been feeling kinda low lately, so I thought I'd try cheering him up." After a pause, she asked, "Care to hang around with me?"

He shook his head. "Can't. Got some leads need running down. I might have to leave town for a few days."

She frowned. "Is there someone else? Because if there is, now's the time to tell me. Before we get too deep into this thing."

"I'm being straight. There's no one," he assured her. "It's this case."

"Where are you going?"

"Nashville."

"When?"

"Depends. Maybe tomorrow or the day after. Not sure yet."

Flashing a grin. "Want company?"

"Hmm. Sounds tempting. But it wouldn't work. I'll

be busy and you'll be bored."

"But think of the fun we'll have at night," she said, holding the grin.

He smiled. "Let's see what happens when I get back to the office."

* * *

While waiting in the Butner Visitors Room for Kleinman, Ruth's thoughts went to the previous evening, when she and Jerzy returned to the inn and fell into each other's arms. And of that morning, when they held each other and traded lingering kisses meant to last until their next meeting up north.

She was smiling to herself, thinking she'd have to push those thoughts from her mind before Leo arrived and started questioning her. It was well past the start of visiting hours when she glanced at the clock across the room. He was never more than a few minutes late, and she wondered if coming two days in a row had caused a problem with the guards. She wanted to inquire across the hall if Leo had been told she was there, but then she wouldn't be allowed to re-enter the Visitors Room. She was stuck there and had to wait.

When Kleinman finally arrived nearly thirty minutes later she was stunned by his demeanor. His face was drawn and he lacked his usual swagger. Even his yarmulke, which always sat squarely atop his head, was askew. And for the first time, his clothes weren't pressed. Rather than focusing on her, he seemed interested in who else was in the room. Even his kiss was perfunctory. Not even her carefully chosen outfit drew a comment. When she offered to retrieve food from the vending machines, he refused.

"What's wrong?" she asked.

Leaning forward and placing his elbows on his knees, he motioned her to do the same, before whispering, "Someone tried to kill me."

She jerked backward, her eyes washing over him. "My God! Are you hurt?"

He shook his head.

"Are you sure?"

"Of course I'm sure."

"What happened?" she said, leaning forward again.

"Someone put glass in my food."

"Glass? Maybe it was an accident."

"It was no accident."

"Are you sure?"

"Yes, damn it. And stop asking if I'm sure."

Still whispering, she said, "How do you know you were the target?"

He looked at her for a long moment, his mouth twitching. "I know."

She reached out to him and, seeing a guard peering into the room, pulled back. Struggling to understand, she said, "Leo, what exactly happened?"

He took a deep breath. "I told you. Someone put glass in my food. Where's that fucking NCIS agent? What the hell's he doing?"

"How'd it happen?"

"For Chrissake, woman! I'm telling you."

"I'm trying to understand, Leo. How can you be sure it was intentional, and why do you think it was intended for you?" The words came rapidly.

"Not once in twenty-five years has there been glass in a kosher meal. It doesn't happen. Our meals come from outside where they don't make such mistakes. Someone inside is responsible."

She shook her head. "How does someone insert glass in kosher meals?"

"Don't be an idiot!" he hissed, spittle gathering in the corners of his mouth. "Just the one meal. The one I was supposed to eat."

"But you didn't eat it?"

"Right. Birnbaum ate it. I gave it to him."

"This isn't making sense. Why'd you give it to him?"

He rolled his eyes and groaned. "He's constipated, so I figured a little glass would clean him out."

Ruth stiffened. "Drop the sarcasm, Leo. I'm not understanding any of this."

"Well, you're not alone," he snapped. "No one in this fucking place does either."

"Okay," she said, splaying her hands and tapping her knees with each word. "From the beginning," she said slowly. "You gave the food to Birnbaum not knowing it was tainted. But you think it was meant for you. Correct?"

"Finally she gets it."

Ruth gave him an icy stare. "What were you doing with Birnbaum's food?"

"He couldn't make it to chow. The flu. So last night I picked up two meals, ate one and brought the other to him."

"You can do that, get two meals?"

He nodded. "With the guards' permission. We can when someone can't make it to the mess hall because he's sick." His tone suggested she was expected to know this. "This morning, I learned he was in the infirmary — a sliver of glass stuck in his esophagus."

She winced. "Thank you, darling. But it still might've been an accident. One piece of glass."

"Damn it! It wasn't *one piece of glass*.

"You just said he swallowed a sliver of glass."

A long sigh. "When they inspected the leftovers they found more fragments. Quite a bit more."

"You didn't say that."

"I said glass in the food, not one piece of glass. Get it?" And when she nodded, he said, "There was glass in the mashed cauliflower. None in the salad, the meat or the cake. Just the cauliflower. A perfect place to conceal it, don't you think? And only in that one meal. The one I picked up. So I asked myself, why would someone want to hurt old Birnbaum, a banker who never harmed a soul? Well, not directly, anyway. And the answer is no one. Which leaves me, the one they call the traitor. The one somebody wants dead, thanks to that crazy woman."

He ran a hand over his mouth, and nodding at the vending machines, said, "Get me a cheese sandwich and a Coke." And when she rose, "Make it two Cokes. My mouth feels like cotton."

When Ruth returned, he tore open the wrapper and bit into the sandwich with a vengeance. "You see what this means?" he said between bites. "If they can put glass in my food they can put anything in it. Even rat poison. How the hell am I going to eat?"

"Did you eat today?" she asked.

He nodded. "I had a knish from the commissary," he said, referring to the kosher food for purchase there. "I'll eat another one tonight. Don't know when I'll go back to the mess hall." Then more to himself, "That's what I'll do. Skip a meal now and then. That'll throw them off balance."

"Poor darling," she said stroking his hand after looking around. "Have you talked with your case manager?"

Kleinman nodded, crumbs falling from his beard. "Of course," he said after washing down his food. "With him, with the correctional counselor *and* the unit manager. Spoke with them all."

"And?"

"And nothing. What're they going to do in this *farkakte* place? What's anybody going to do?"

"They didn't do *anything*?"

"They said, if I wanted, I could go into the SHU."

She thought a moment. "Maybe you should. Just for a while. Till they catch this woman."

"How many times must I say it? I'm not going into solitary! That's what she wants. First she wants me dead, and if that fails she wants me in solitary. Well it isn't going to happen. I'd rather be dead."

"Please, Leo, don't talk like that."

"What are my options?"

"I'd rather have you alive in the Special Housing Unit."

"That's not a life. Locked up twenty-three hours."

"Have they done anything else?" she asked.

"The usual. A shakedown, but found nothing to connect anyone. I coulda told them that."

"What happened to Birnbaum?"

"They extracted the sliver. He's fine. The rest, they say, he'll pass. It turns out ground glass rarely causes internal injuries. The bowel handles it without a problem."

Ruth clicked her tongue. "Who would've guessed."

"With my luck, *I'd* have a problem."

"What're you talking about, with *your luck*? It was your luck that Birnbaum got the glass. He should have your luck."

He was about to say something, but shoved the remainder of his sandwich in his mouth instead, then popped open the second can and took a long gulp.

"Tell me how it's going with the super sleuth?" he said after swallowing.

"He has the envelopes and is on his way north with

them. He didn't say it outright, but they may provide a useful clue. I'll call him after I return."

"Let's hope so." Then, after another swig, he asked, "Is he good in bed?"

"Can we not go down that road? I'm doing what you asked me to do."

"I just want to know if you enjoy spreading your legs for him."

"What does that have to do with anything?"

"Is he a good fuck?" And when she didn't respond, "Well?"

"Yes, he's very good. Okay? Does that make you feel better?"

He shrugged. "Beh." Then, his mouth twitching, he said, "Tell me about it."

"I will not."

"How often do you do it? Does he make you scream?"

"Stop! This is perverse."

Another shrug. "I have to get my jollies somehow. I may as well get them vicariously." And when she fell silent, "Do you like him?"

"Don't be ridiculous. Jerzy means nothing to me. You're the only one I care about. My thoughts are always with you."

"So it's Jerzy, eh? Not Agent Shore."

"Leo, you're being foolish. He's a *boychik*. Easily manipulated. You shouldn't concern yourself."

"A boychik, eh?" he said screwing up his face at the endearment. "To my parents and my sisters I was a boychik, and to my rabbi, as well. They loved me. To you, boychik means nothing. Why don't I believe you?"

Ruth was shaking her head. "Darling," she pleaded, "wash those thoughts from your mind. My heart belongs to you. Only you."

"Meanwhile, the boychik has your body. I hope you

use it wisely. My wife acting like a *shlooche*…"

Ruth drew back, her eyes widening. "How dare you!" she said attracting looks from those around them. "This was *your* idea." Then, lowering her voice again, she clenched her jaw and said, "You're one helluva man. You know that? The big *choshever mench*—Israel's super hero—throws his wife out there like a piece of meat and then has the nerve to call her a slut. How proud you must feel."

Kleinman was no longer listening. His gaze and thoughts were elsewhere. Shaking his head, he mumbled, "Gotta do something. Can't let this go on. This business with the glass is the beginning. Next time the putz will get it right. And if he doesn't get me, someone else will."

"Leo. Look at me, Leo." He looked up and she said, "It'll be all right." Though she wondered if it really would.

"Ha. Easy for you to say."

When it was time to go, Ruth ignored the knot in her stomach while kissing him and passing on the drug-filled capsule. For the first time, their kiss was tendered without much feeling.

Later, while driving to Maryland, she thought of Jerzy and decided maybe she did like him.

NINETEEN

After talking with Theo, I decided the best thing to do was head for Nashville, scout the area and see what I could learn. I flew out the following morning, checked into the Marriott Vanderbilt and, using a grid I developed based on zip codes taken from Kleinman's envelopes, I crisscrossed my way through town, starting out by the airport in the 37214 area. I didn't know what I was looking for, and wasn't sure I'd know it when I spotted it. Still, I was fairly certain there was a pattern—something that repeatedly drew the letter writer to the same areas—and I meant to find it.

Having completed a day and a half of circular driving with no results, I was back in my room contemplating the ceiling from my bed when Sarah called.

"I'm lonesome," she pined.

We had spoken shortly after she returned home from Butner. Now, hearing her voice made me realize how much I missed her. "That makes two of us," I replied, feeling sorry for myself.

"What's the matter, no luck running down your lead?"

"I feel like a rat in a maze," I said. "Nothing but dead ends."

"Sounds like you could use some company."

"You read my mind."

"Then why don't you come pick me up. I'm at the airport."

I jumped up, swinging my feet off the bed. "You serious?"

"Come see for yourself."

"I'm on my way!" I said, and headed for my car.

She was waiting outside the terminal, looking as alluring as ever, without a wrinkle in her clothes or a hair out of place. I pulled up, hopped out and wrapped my arms around her. "Welcome to Nashville."

She smiled. "Nice to be here." Once in the car, she said, "I'm famished. Know any good spots the locals favor?"

"You're in luck," I said, and twenty minutes later we were west of town pulling into the Lions Head Shopping Center, home of Dalts American Grill. "The concierge at the hotel recommended it," I said. "Ate here yesterday. Not fancy, but the best home cooking around, I'm told."

Once seated, I took her hand and said, "I can't believe you're here."

"Neither can I. I mean, one minute I'm bouncing off the walls thinking about us and the next, here I am."

"Maybe you'll bring me luck."

"I've been known to do that," she said.

After dinner, when she suggested having a drink somewhere before heading to the hotel, I asked the young waitress if she had any recommendations.

"You're smart, you'll stay away from the honkytonks on Broadway and go here instead," she said, scribbling down the name and address of a nearby place.

I looked at the paper. "The Patterson House."

"You'll love it. Best bartenders and drinks around." Adding as an afterthought, "Don't bother looking for signs. There ain't none. Just plug the address in your GPS." And as we headed for the door, she called, "Try the Juliet and Romeo."

She was right. Not only was there no sign, nothing distinguished the place from its neighbors. Sited at a Y intersection, the Patterson House was a nondescript gray house squeezed in among similar single family homes. The only parking was on the street, and I found a spot midway down the block, beyond a neighborhood food market. While climbing the concrete steps, I prepared my apology to the homeowners for interrupting their evening if this wasn't the place. But it was, and we were greeted by a tuxedoed host who ushered us into a vestibule lined with bookshelves and large enough to accommodate ten or so couples comfortably.

"Ah, we don't have reservations," I said.

"No problem," he said. "It's first come, first served. No exceptions."

There were three couples ahead of us, and I asked, "How long's the wait?"

He smiled. "About ten minutes. Fifteen at most." Just then, the heavy gray velvet floor-to-ceiling curtains parted and a young couple shuffled out, allowing a momentary glimpse of the happy crowd inside, and for an instant I felt like I was flying coach and getting a peek at the more privileged in first class.

By the time it was our turn to be escorted inside I had scanned the titles of several shelves of books and read the plaque beneath the large portrait of the bar's namesake, former Governor Malcolm R. Patterson, who, according to the plaque, had courageously vetoed the return of statewide Prohibition only to have his veto overridden by the state legislature.

After checking his seating chart, our host parted the curtains and led us inside into a spacious paneled dark chestnut room accented with ivory and silver wallpaper, which Sarah later described as Great Gatsby chic. "Welcome to our speakeasy," he announced while leading us to two seats at the enormous square bar.

"Aren't there any tables?" I said.

"Trust me, sir, you want to sit at the bar. No one asks for a table. This is where it's happening."

I looked at Sarah, who shrugged. "Your call."

"The bar it is," I said, and was glad for it, as we settled into two comfortable black leather covered chairs. The bartenders, or mixologists, as they preferred, were pros who clearly relished crafting any and all orders with a showman's flair from the hundreds of liquors and eyedropper apothecary bottles filled with syrups and bitters.

"Hi, I'm Bo," our bartender said, handing us a thick menu of such odd named drinks as Bacon Manhattan, Maple Nut Manhattan and The Brave Die Once, all listed by liquor type. "First time here?" he asked. And when we nodded, he suggested taking our time, which we did.

"We need your help," I confessed when he returned. "I've never heard of most of these."

"I'm not surprised. We concoct our recipes right here in our mixology lab, tweaking the menu every three months."

"You're serious?" I asked.

"Absolutely. These are some of the popular drinks," he said, going down the list.

His recitation did little to lessen our confusion and so, recalling the waitress's advice, Sarah ordered the Juliet and Romeo, a mix of gin, lime, mint, cucumber and rose water. Staying with gin, and liking the name, I went with the Daisy Bae, a concoction of tea-infused gin, lime, Campari, homemade raspberry syrup and grapefruit bitters. Both drinks were tasty, tasty enough that we consumed more than we intended.

We had arrived soon after dusk and didn't leave until nearly eleven. The evening air was cool and refreshing, and I kept the windows down as we drove. I took a detour back to the hotel, stopping at the life-size replica of the Parthenon in Centennial Park, which I had visited the previous day. Lit up, the structure served as a magnet for locals and tourists alike.

We walked around the massive structure, stealing kisses in the shadows, each embrace more heated than the previous one, so that by the time we returned to the car we were both anxious to reach the hotel.

I awoke the next morning before Sarah, threw on a robe and stepped onto the balcony. The broad Vanderbilt campus across the street was quiet in the pre-dawn hours. Off to my right, I saw the flashing lights of an approaching ambulance about a mile down West End Avenue, its siren, growing louder as it neared, prompting a string of early commuters to pull to the curb as it overtook them and headed for Vanderbilt Hospital. As if on cue, a second ambulance came from downtown and I tried calculating which would arrive first. In that instant, the puzzle of the zip codes came together. While crisscrossing town, I had passed several hospitals and medical centers. It made perfect sense. By now, all *Liberty* survivors were senior citizens likely requiring some degree of care. The anonymous letter writer had to be posting her letters while delivering a family member to his medical appointments.

I rushed inside and checked the time. It was too early to call Theo. But it wasn't too early to retrace those same routes. I took a hurried shower, and when I emerged Sarah was sitting up, the covers below her waist.

"You're up early. Come back to bed," she cooed,

kicking away the covers.

"Not now. I gotta go," I said.

Frowning, she came over and pressed against me. "At this hour?"

"I think I figured out a link to the letters. But I have to be sure."

She smiled and rubbed up against me. "See, I told you I'd bring you luck. May I come?"

I was anxious to go. "Why don't you stay here and relax? I'll just be driving around the city."

"I'll be ready in a few minutes," she said heading for the shower. "Get us coffee from the lobby. I'll be dressed before you're back."

She was blow drying her hair when I returned.

"What is it?" she asked as I set her coffee down. "This link?"

"Hospitals. Medical centers." Noting her confusion, I said, "I think the woman's posting her letters when she takes the person she's caring for—likely a *Liberty* crewman—to town for treatment."

She looked intrigued. "How'd you figure that?"

"It just came to me. It's the best explanation I can come up with. And now, I have to be sure."

"Then, what?"

"If I'm right, we narrow it down."

"We?" she said with some excitement.

"Me and the guys back at the office." I gulped my coffee. "Let's go."

As we passed through the lobby, she said, "Rather than just tag along, I'd like to help. Really."

"I'll keep it in mind," I said, patting her arm.

For the next several hours we followed my zip code grid in and around Nashville, noting every hospital and medical center we came across. When we finished, we had identified three hospitals and a medical center, not including the VA Hospital on the Vanderbilt campus, where I intended to begin my search.

It was time for lunch and I found a steak and oyster restaurant downtown near the river—The Southern—and sent Sarah inside to get us a table while I phoned Theo.

"I think I'm on to something," I said the instant he answered.

"Who is this?"

"Always the clown," I replied, and quickly laid out my findings.

"A tip of the hat to you, old chum."

"I need you to contact the National Personnel Records Center in St. Louis. See if they can ID former *Liberty* crewmen residing in the Nashville area."

"Just drop everything and call St. Louis?"

"Theo, I'm serious."

He laughed. "You're already my top priority."

"Really? How'd that happen?"

"You don't know?"

"Know what?"

"According to the warden, there was an attempt on your boy's life. At least that's what Kleinman's claiming. The warden isn't so sure."

"When? What happened?"

"There was glass in one of his kosher meals," Theo explained. "But instead of eating it, he passed it on to another inmate," he said, before going on about how the mix-up occurred. "Both men are okay. The warden isn't ruling out an accident, he's looking into the company that prepares the meals. Meanwhile, he ordered a lockdown and a shakedown. Nothing so far."

"Where's Kleinman?" I asked.

"Still in place, but being very careful what he puts in his mouth," I hear.

I thanked him, and said to call if he learned anything more.

"What's wrong?" Sarah asked when I caught up with her. "You're looking flustered."

I took the seat across from her. "The guy I'm supposed to be protecting. Someone may've tried to kill him."

She blanched. "Again!"

"What? What do you mean *again*?"

"I… uh…"

"What do you know? Is there something you're not telling me?"

"Don't be silly. What happened?" she said, deflecting my question.

"Never mind what happened. Why'd you say *again*?"

She took a sip of water. "I spoke with my brother before coming here and he mentioned being in lockdown because one of the prisoners ate some glass, and maybe it was intentional. I don't remember his name, but when he said he's a convicted traitor, I figured it was the case you're working. So when you said what you did, I assumed someone had tried again, which meant my brother's in lockdown again. Is that what happened?"

"No. I was referring to the incident with the glass. I only just learned of it. Your grapevine's more efficient than mine. I should be talking with your brother."

She laughed. "I doubt he'd talk to you. Unless, of course, you can get him an early release."

"Not likely. But if you hear anything more about this prisoner, tell me."

"Okay," she said with a nod. "What's his name? The traitor?"

What the hell, I thought, knowing his name won't change things. "Leo Kleinman."

"That's it. I remember, now," she said. "What did he do?"

"Sold a ton of military secrets to Israel back in the eighties. His name's been in the news lately in connection with a presidential pardon if Israel agrees to a sit-down with the Palestinians."

She was nodding. "I read something about that. You think it'll happen?"

I shrugged. "Anything's possible in today's world."

"Sounds as though you disapprove."

"Wouldn't you? He did irreparable harm. As far as I'm concerned, they should've hanged the bastard when they had the chance."

She didn't respond.

The check came and I looked at my watch. "I'll drop you off at the hotel."

"No. Let me come with you."

"There's nothing for you to do. It's routine police work."

"If I get bored I'll take a taxi to the hotel. Besides, I bring you luck."

We arrived at the VA Hospital about twenty-five minutes later.

"Wait here," I said, outside the administrator's office. I was back a minute later.

"That was quick."

"They directed me to another office," I said, as we headed for the elevator. "I hope they aren't giving me the runaround."

I left Sarah outside the Privacy Office, went inside and, showing my badge, identified myself to the director, a woman about my age.

"Meg Adams," she said, extending her hand.

I was about to explain why I was there when I spotted the soapstone carving of a three-legged frog on her desk—a duplicate of the one on my desk. As I looked around I saw other items indicating a well-laid-out feng shui space: small pieces of crystal quartz set around the office at intervals to multiply the positive chi flow, two ferns to clean the air, the eight-sided Bagua mirror to deflect influences of negative energy, and her correctly positioned desk and chairs. I had stumbled upon a kindred soul. "Aah, the positive *chi*," I said, soaking in the energy.

She smiled. "You're familiar with feng shui?"

"Very. I'm a disciple," I said, and went on about failing to convert my boss and co-workers.

"Me, too. I've given up. Now, I simply invite them in and let them feel the energy. If they're astute enough to pick it up, I enlighten them. Otherwise," she shrugged, "their loss."

"You're a wise woman," I said. "I haven't reached that level yet. I still have that missionary zeal and it's driving my boss nuts."

She nodded. "They called ahead and told me you were on your way and that you're seeking patient information. I must warn you, Agent Shore, we're restricted on how we can help."

"I know. I'm painfully aware of the regs protecting patient privacy," I said, and shared my experiences while working spousal and child abuse cases years earlier. "Those were not happy days, but I did learn there's some flexibility with requests from valid law enforcement agencies."

"If the information doesn't adversely affect the patient," she reminded me.

"Right. It won't," I promised. "The individual we're seeking would be classified as a witness and not a suspect."

"In that case, what is it you'd like from us, Agent Shore?"

I handed her my list. "There's a good chance one

of these Navy crewmen from the USS *Liberty* is an outpatient here. I'd be grateful if you would check the names against your files."

She looked it over and raised an eyebrow. "There are close to a hundred names here. I don't have the manpower to devote to this. Certainly not in a timely fashion."

I thought a moment. "Would it help if I provided assistance?"

She considered it. "I suppose we can make an exception," she said, adding, "As long as we comply with the law."

"My assistant is outside. May I bring her in?" She nodded and I excused myself. "Be right back."

"Sarah, I'm taking you up on that offer to help," I said, and quickly explained the problem, telling her I still had several places on my list to check out. "You feel comfortable doing this?"

She grinned. "I'm looking forward to it."

A moment later, I said to the director, "I'd like you to meet Special Agent Sarah Grayson."

TWENTY

Lou Chatham took Tom Kelly aside, away from the other inmates in the yard. "I thought you had street smarts, friend. I've seen guys killed for what you didn't do."

Kelly shook his head. "How the hell was I supposed to know you gotta take one leg out?" he said through swollen lips and loose teeth. "Fuckin' crazy rule."

"Crazy on the outside," Chatham conceded. "Not in here."

Kelly didn't reply.

"Damn greenhorns. I don't know how you survive."

"Nobody told me," Kelly insisted.

"You have to be told everything?" Chatham said, his patience wearing thin. "It's common sense. Take one leg out of your pants while you shit. Shows you're ready to defend yourself. It happens again, you'll get your throat slit. I guarantee it."

Kelly looked up at his mentor. "It won't."

Chatham snorted. "They'll get you with something else now that you're marked."

Kelly frowned. "Marked? Whatdya mean?"

"That stupidity showed you're a pushover." Swinging an open hand toward the others in the yard, he said,

"They know it, and now the sharks are circling."

Kelly clutched Chatham's sleeve. "You can't be serious!"

"'Fraid so, friend," he said pulling away. "You fucked up."

"But... The Brotherhood... You said you'd look out for me. Take care of things."

"That's when we thought you had what it takes."

"And one screw-up in the john makes you think I don't?"

"It isn't what I think. It's what they think," he said, nodding toward the yard again. This joint's overcrowded. Not enough COs to protect everyone. Which means guys like you are going to suffer. That's just how it is."

"But..."

"There are no buts. Those suckers out there fear us because we're strong," he said thumping his chest. "And we're strong because we don't waste energy coddling every Sweet Suzie coming through the gate," he said, thumping Kelly's chest.

"I ain't no Sweet Suzie!" Kelly protested, working to maintain his balance.

"You sure act like one."

"You can't leave me hanging out there! They know you helped me. If they see we ain't friends no more..." Then, steadying his voice and squaring his shoulders, he declared, "I'm taking down the next fucker comes at me. You'll see." And when Chatham didn't respond, "Don't count me out." Then, wanting to resolve this before the four o'clock headcount, he glanced at his watch, and said, "I hung with you on the walking track. Stood with you against them niggers. I backed you."

"I didn't forget."

"That's gotta count for something."

Chatham, offering a slow nod, replied, "It did. At the time."

"Well you can't just forget about it."

Chatham studied him. "I'll think about it."

Kelly surveyed the yard. Knots of men were ambling toward their units for the headcount. "When...?" he said as Chatham walked away.

"I'll let you know," he said over his shoulder.

"I can handle one-on-one," Kelly said, pursuing him. "Anybody tries something I'll get the bastard," he assured him. "But," he said twitching, "more come at me, I'm fucked." Lacking a response, he repeated, "You can't leave me hanging, Lew. It ain't right."

Chatham stopped and turned. "Meet me at the walking track after dinner," he said, and strode away.

"Right!" Kelly called after him. "See you then. Right after chow."

* * *

Kelly was pacing beside the track when Chatham approached.

Let's walk," Chatham said stepping onto the asphalt.

"Sure," Kelly replied, hurrying to catch up.

"Here's the deal," Chatham told him. "We'll let you in, and you'll have our protection."

"Great! I swear, you won't be sorry..."

"Not so fast, friend. This isn't the Rotary Club. You don't *just come in*."

"Yeah. I, uh, figured that. I gotta do something, right? Whatever. Just tell me."

Chatham stopped and looked hard at Kelly. "You don't have the slightest idea what you're agreeing to."

"It don't matter. I'll do what it takes."

"We'll see."

"I mean it. Whatever it takes."

"Our code is *blood in-blood out*. You know what that means?" When Kelly shook his head, Chatham asked, "What do you think it means?"

Kelly creased his brow. "Uh… Some kinda blood oath?"

"It means," he said holding Kelly's gaze, "you have to spill blood to get in. You have to kill somebody. That's the *blood in* part."

Kelly swallowed. "I never killed no one," he said, his voice cracking.

"It's easy," Chatham assured him. "Nothing to it."

"Who… who do I gotta kill?"

"*Blood out* means you're in for life, not just while you're inside. There's only one way out." Chatham waited for Kelly's response, and when it didn't come, he asked, "You sure you got the cojones for this? 'Cause if you don't…"

They had paused beside the track's grass infield, allowing others to pass—some strolling in pairs, others pumping their fists and grunting as if in a foot race—no one turning their way, but Kelly felt their gaze nonetheless.

"Well?" Chatham pressed him.

Eyeing a group of black laundry workers across the field, Kelly drew a breath and thrust his chin out. "I can handle it. Who do I hafta whack?"

Chatham smiled. "A Jew."

TWENTY-ONE

I drove east, away from Vanderbilt, across the Cumberland River toward Donelson Medical Center, where I began my search days earlier. Along the way, I spotted the Tennessee Law Enforcement Training Academy and was reminded of Al Eastman, a fellow student whom I'd met while attending a Forensic Tracking course at the FBI Academy in Quantico. As the only bachelors in our small class, we tended to drift away from the others in the evenings, heading north to scout the pubs in Alexandria or south to Fredericksburg as the mood struck us. It had been several years, and I wondered if Al was still teaching here.

"Morning," I said to the young uniformed clerk manning the front desk, while showing my badge and ID. "Can you tell me if Al Eastman is still on the faculty?"

"He's Supervisor of Training," she said.

"Would it be possible to see him?" I asked, and waited while she phoned his office.

Moments later, Eastman, a twenty-year police veteran, who was taller and broader than I, came bounding across the lobby, a wide toothy grin below his thick moustache. Except for his fleshy veined nose, which was more bulbous than I recalled, he was still the same rugged looking guy. Seeing that mischievous gleam in his eyes, and the gal behind the desk suddenly perking up, I felt certain he was still a force with the ladies. He was coming at me full gallop, and I braced myself.

"Iceman, you old rascal!" he shouted, lifting me in a bear hug. "You haven't changed!" His booming voice hung in my ears as he released me. Then came the balled fist to my shoulder. "How long's it been? Four, five years?"

"About that," I said, steadying myself. I considered delivering a counterpunch but, recalling Eastman's fondness for sparring, decided against it. "You're looking pretty fit yourself."

"Gotta keep the women happy," he said, pounding his flat stomach. "Ain't that right, Clarice?" he said, shooting a grin at the clerk, who had been doing her best to look occupied, and who now appeared uncertain if Eastman's comment warranted a response.

"I see you've been promoted," I said before she made up her mind. "Congratulations."

"Yeah, well, shit happens. And you?"

I said I was still working cold cases.

"What about the skirts?" he said elbowing me. "Still chasing 'em?"

Feeling the receptionist's gaze, I shrugged and said, "Occasionally."

"Occasionally, my ass, you scallywag." I saw the fist, but I was too slow. This one caught me in the rib cage.

By now there was no point pretending to ignore us, so when Eastman turned to the young woman, and warned her, "Watch this guy, Clarice. He's trouble," she offered me a gracious smile.

It was time to move on, and I asked, "You going to invite me inside?"

"Sure. Sure. Come on," he said throwing a beefy arm around my shoulder. "What brings you to these parts?" he said, steering me back to his office. Before I could reply, he was back in Quantico, recalling past misdeeds. "Remember the gal we met in that roadside joint? Hailed from one of those nearby horse farms?"

I nodded. "The one with the skintight jeans, fancy boots and pierced tongue." I recalled her vividly. Having spotted her the moment we strolled into the place, I had wasted little time sliding onto the bar stool beside her while Al scouted the bar. She was slender and tall, quite tall, and easy to talk to, and I was certain I'd hit the mother lode that evening. That is until Al sidled over and, learning she was an equestrian, held her captive with tales of his family's horse farm in Kentucky.

"That's the one! Gawd, she was somethin'," he said. "Would you believe thinking about her still gives me a jolt? Like them poor souls with dead weenies get from them Viagra pills. What a woman."

I laughed. "Do you also think about you two disappearing around midnight, leaving me with the bar tab?"

He cleared his throat. "Can't say as I do." Then, closing his eyes and shivering, he said, "She could teach a contortionist tricks. Hot damn, that was one helluva night."

"Not for me," I said as he directed me past his secretary and into his office.

Kicking the door shut with his heel, he said, "I believe you would've done the same had you been quicker on the draw."

"Guess we'll never know."

"Enough of that," he said, dropping into his chair. "So, what brings the Iceman to our fair city?"

"Glad you asked," I said, and gave him a rundown

about my case, concluding with the zip codes placing the anonymous female letter writer in the Nashville area, and my hunch about the hospitals.

"You got yourself an interesting one, there. If you're right you've done some fine detective work. 'Cept if it was me," he said, lowering his voice, "I'd be dragging my feet so as to give them scoundrels in Butner enough time to kill the traitor."

"That might still happen. Someone's already made one attempt," I said, and told him about the incident with the glass.

"Heh. You may be running out of time," he said, as if that were a good thing.

"Which is why I've got to run down this woman and find out what else she's got up her sleeve."

Eastman shook his head. "To each his own." Then, in a more conciliatory tone, he reached out, saying, "Lemme see what you've come up with." Scanning my list, he said, "There may be more. Stay put." Then, bouncing up he went out to confer with his secretary, and when he returned, he was waving a sheet of paper. "Here you are, pal. These here health facilities also fall within your zip codes."

I took it and read down the list.

Tri-Star Summit Medical Center
Bradlee Medical Center
Medical Arts Center
St. Thomas Doctors Medical Center
Middle Tennessee Mental Health Institute

"Beautiful. You may've solved this case," I said.

Eastman slapped his desk. "Good! Let's celebrate tonight and corral us some heifers across the river. I know some swell spots in the honkytonk district. It'll be easy pickins."

I shook my head. "Can't do that."

His grin fell away. "Whatdaya mean?"

"I mean, I'll have to pass."

He raised an eyebrow. "Say what?" When I told him I was travelling with Sarah, he shook his head and frowned. "What the hell were you thinking bringing a ham sandwich to a buffet? Nashville lays claim to some of the finest lookin' women 'round these parts. You're slippin', my friend."

"She's no ham sandwich," I countered. "This one's special."

He narrowed his eyes. "Maybe so. But you know what they say about variety." And when I didn't reply, he said, "Well then I suppose you oughta be hightailing it if you're going to run down that letter writer."

"I really should," I said, and thanked him for his help.

When we reached the reception desk, he handed me his card, telling me to call if I needed anything else. I said I would, and hurried to my car.

Using my GPS, I ran through the list, explaining my mission to each administrator and office manager. All were cooperative, and I soon singled out a former *Liberty* crewman from my list of survivors residing in the region who had been seen by physicians and therapists in the area within a day of the postmarked dates on Kleinman's envelopes. I had hit a home run. By the time I concluded my search, I not only had his name, but his address in Franklin, a town about twenty miles south of Nashville, as well. Now, all I needed was one more piece of information.

I phoned Eastman. "Al, one more favor, please."

"It'll cost you," he said with a boyish chuckle.

"How much?"

"A night on the town next time I'm up your way. That is, if your woman'll let you out."

"You got it," I said. "We'll hit every hot spot in

town. But first I need you to run a check on someone in Franklin." I gave him the name and address I'd come up with, saying, "With his ailments he's probably living with his caregiver, and my guess is she's our letter writer. Can you get me her name?"

"That's all?" And when I said yes, he laughed. "Better start making plans for our night out. I'll have it for you in no time."

Sure enough, Eastman got back to me in less than thirty minutes with a name, saying he got it through a reverse address search from the DMV. I thanked him again and said I was looking forward to seeing him in D.C. soon.

"Her name's Hattie Mullin," I told Theo as I drove back to Vanderbilt. "Pass it on to the warden at Butner. See if she shows up on the visitors list or if she'd been an employee in the last year or so."

I was riding high when I strode into Meg Adam's office at the VA hospital. And, as I learned, so was Sarah, who, with Meg's help, had narrowed her list of crewmen to three names, including my guy. I discounted the other two since neither name had popped up at any of the other facilities across the river.

I thanked Meg Adams for her assistance, and we left.

"Where to now, Kimosabe?" Sarah asked once we were outside.

"South about twenty miles," I said.

*   *   *

The house was six miles south of Brentwood, just outside the Franklin city limits on Bremond Street. It sat on an unfenced lot about sixty feet back from a two-lane stretch of county road. Like its neighbors, it was a modest rancher, this one brown brick with a low roof and a long, narrow driveway leading to a carport and, farther back, a faded green and white utility shed. A wheelchair ramp had been built over the three steps leading to the porch, where a faded American flag hung limp in the still afternoon. There was a bone-dry concrete birdbath set between two shade trees in the front yard, and a TV satellite dish anchored to the asphalt roof.

Except for the van in the carport, there didn't appear to be anyone home or, for that matter, at any of the other homes we'd passed.

I parked on the shoulder of the road, just beyond the weathered mailbox. "Better wait here," I said.

Sarah laughed. "Uh-uh. No way you're leaving your special agent partner out here."

"For backup," I told her.

"Yeah. Right. I'm coming with you," she said, jumping out before I turned off the engine.

I shrugged and followed her to the front door.

A frail woman with stooped shoulders answered my knock, cracking the door enough to peer at us through tired eyes.

"Hattie Mullin?" I asked.

"Who are you?"

I produced my ID, figuring it sufficed for both of us, saying, "Ma'am, we're here about the letters you've been sending to Mr. Leo Kleinman."

Her only response was to purse her lips for a long moment. Then nodding, she stood back, opening the door wider. "You better come inside."

The house was closed up and musty, and we followed her through a dark, heavily curtained living room, past a stripped down hospital bed, idle oxygen tanks and a folded wheelchair. Sidestepping a sofa and coffee table, both pressed into a corner, we passed through the dining room, its table and sideboard cluttered with assorted medications and paraphernalia and stacks of hospital and insurance forms, to an enclosed rear porch, where the stale odor was less intense and where the woman looked younger in the late afternoon sun than I had thought her to be.

We no sooner sat when she apologized for the disorder, explaining that her father had recently passed away and she was still sorting through a tangle of paperwork.

"Was your father a crewman aboard USS *Liberty*?" I asked.

She moistened her lips, said he was and, without prompting, related a lengthy tale of how he had acquired the injuries that led to years of debilitating ailments. It was an unemotional recitation that neither required nor elicited comments from us. We simply sat there as the sun crept across the bare floor, listening to the woman unburden herself.

When she finished, I asked, "Is that why you're targeting Leo Kleinman, Ms. Mullin? Because of what your father went through?"

She looked at me, blinked and said, "I'm not targeting him. I don't even know the man."

"But the letters," I said. "We know they were written by a woman and then mailed near a medical facility your father visited. Further, the postmarks coincide with the dates of those visits. There doesn't appear to be anyone else but you."

"Oh, I mailed them, all right," she conceded, "but I didn't write them."

"Well then, who did?"

A thin smile crossed her lips. "You need to leave now."

TWENTY-TWO

Chatham leaned into Kelly and, dropping all pretense of affability, warned, "Don't let me down, you little fucker."

In the brief time Kelly had known him, Chatham had only used such harsh language when baiting blacks or referring to them, and it rattled him having the big man address him this way. "No! I promise," he said, his voice cracking under the taller man's gaze. "I'm in this a hundred percent."

They were standing away from the others, in the shadow of the admin building. By rights, Kelly should not have been sweating in the cool, early autumn afternoon, but he was; a nervous, foul sweat that couldn't be ignored. He swallowed hard and again assured his only source of protection. "All you gotta do is point him out," he said. "I'll do the rest."

Chatham looked hard at him. "You fuck up and it's both our heads. First yours, then mine. You got that?"

"I... I won't screw it up," Kelly insisted. "I'm solid."

Chatham nodded. "We'll see."

Kelly licked his lips. "Where's the mark?"

"The little shit's housed in Clemson Unit."

"What's his name?"

"Later."

"Why can't you tell me now?"

Chatham shook his head. "You still don't get it, do you?"

"Get what?"

"I don't know you from Jack."

Kelly looked stunned. "Whataya mean? I thought we was friends."

"What have I been telling you? There are no friends in here. Today's friend is tomorrow's rat."

"I'm no rat. You can trust me."

"Not a chance."

"Hey. Didn't I stand right there with you on the track that first day?"

Chatham laughed. "You stood with me because you were too scared to walk away."

"Bullshit!" Kelly protested, squaring his shoulders. "I was ready to back you."

"Relax. If I were you I'da done the same. But that don't mean squat now. I tell you the target's name, the next thing I'm standing in front of the warden and you're out of here, shipped off to another joint with a reduced sentence. Happens all the time, guys ratting out a buddy. The only ones I trust are my brothers. And I'm not making an exception for you."

"But…"

"Forget it. Not until you're in. Until then, you're another potential rat. That's how it is and that's how it stays."

Kelly felt compelled to defend himself. "I been straight with you and the others," he said shifting his weight. "You know that."

"Doesn't make a difference. You're not in till you spill blood."

Kelly swallowed hard. "When do I hit this mother?"

Chatham studied him for a long beat. "You sure you're up for it? Because if you're not, this is the time to speak up. We'll go our separate ways, no hard feelings."

"I said I was up for it."

"Saying and doing are two different things."

"I'm tellin' you I'm ready."

"Good," Chatham said. "It's tonight. After dinner. That work for you?"

"Tonight? Yeah, sure." After a moment, he asked, "How am I supposed to do it?"

"Shank him."

"Shank him?"

"Ever use one?"

"I…"

"It's not like shooting someone. You have to get up close, close enough to smell his breath," Chatham said moving in on him. "And you have to be quick. You get one chance." Chatham's voice was slow, his gaze deliberate. "You play poker?" When Kelly nodded, he said, "So you know about tells."

"Tells? Sure. Everybody knows about 'em."

"You can't act nervous or anxious, 'cause that's a tell. The key," he stressed, "is staying cool, but not overly cool, because that's a tell, too. You with me?"

"Yeah. Cool but not too cool."

"Good," Chatham said. "And you have to watch your target without him reading your eyes. Where you look and how you look also sends signals."

Kelly was hanging on every word, his eyes fixed on Chatham.

"If he suspects something, he'll keep his distance, or he'll put somebody between you—another con or a guard—to keep you from reaching him. You can't get too close. I saw a guy drop someone with a pencil because he got too close. Got him right here," he said pressing a finger into Kelly's larynx. When Kelly flinched, he said, "You don't have to worry about that with your guy. He's old and slow, but he isn't stupid. So, what you do is surprise him. Nail him when he isn't expecting it—right in the heart. You know where the heart is?"

Kelly blinked. "I ain't a moron."

"Yeah, well, don't forget it. I've seen guys hit everywhere but the heart. Like they were attacking a goddamn piñata."

"Where do I get the shiv?"

Chatham grimaced. "Shank. I said *shank*."

"Okay. Shank."

"You know the difference?"

Kelly felt his face warm. How the hell was he going to kill this guy if he didn't know one weapon from another?

"A shiv, my little friend, is a knife," he said, bringing his arm around Kelly's neck and pulling him toward him while pushing his head back. "You cut or slice with a knife." His finger slicing across Kelly's extended neck. "The way this hit's going down you won't have time to slice the mook. That's why the shank—long and tapered, like an icepick. You do it quick. One stab and you're out of there. Like this," he said, jabbing his fist into Kelly's chest.

"Then what? Leave it in him?"

"No! You walk away and you drop it. You don't look back and you don't run. You walk like nothing happened and bing, you release it."

"Just drop it? What about my prints?"

"Don't worry. It'll disappear." He cracked a smile. "It's like that line in *The Godfather*, where Clemenza tells Lampone, 'Leave the gun. Take the cannoli.' You saw the movie?" And when Kelly shook his head, the smile faded.

* * *

It never occurred to Kelly to question why there was always a place for him at one of the brothers' tables when he emerged from the mess line with his tray that week. He was just pleased to be in the brotherhood's tent. This evening, he slid in beside Chatham, who had kept him close that afternoon.

"It's not going to get better any time soon," Chatham was telling the others as Kelly joined them. "Budgets are being cut…"

"What's not getting better? What budgets?" Kelly asked, raising his voice enough to be heard over the cacophony.

Chatham turned to him and said, "The Bureau of Prisons is operating on the cheap because of budget cuts, which is why there aren't as many guards."

Kelly shook his head. "Not as many guards?"

Chatham nodded. "Fewer than before," he said as if that were explanation enough.

But it wasn't for Kelly, who continued looking puzzled. "I don't know. I see them everywhere."

Chatham forced a smile. "You haven't been around long enough to know the difference."

"So what's your point?" Kelly asked.

"My point, my friend, is the staff shortage is going to work for us tonight."

"How?"

"Nobody'll be around when you do the hit."

"How's that possible?" Kelly said, a spoonful of rice and beans hovering over his tray.

"You ask too many fuckin' questions," said the skinhead who'd been scowling at Kelly since he joined them. "Why you gotta ask so many questions?"

"Lay off," Chatham said. "How else is he going to

learn?" Then turning to Kelly, he asked, "Why the long face?"

"Can't you tell?" the skinhead said. "He's scared."

"That right?" Chatham said. "You scared?"

"I ain't scared," Kelly said without looking up from his tray.

"It's his first hit," Chatham said to the others. "He'll be okay." Then, to Kelly, "Here. Take this. You'll feel better."

Kelly looked at the small blue pill in Chatham's hand. "What's that?"

"It'll calm your nerves. Take it now. It'll kick in later when you need it. Go on. You'll be glad you did," he said, sliding it over to him.

"Take the fuckin' thing," the skinhead said when Kelly hesitated.

Chatham offered a reassuring smile. "It'll do you good."

Kelly did as he was told, gulping it down with his milk. "Ain't it time somebody tells me who I'm supposed to hit?" he said.

"Perfect timing. Here he comes," Chatham said, nodding toward the rear of the mess line. "The pudgy kike with the gray beard and the beanie coming in now."

Kelly looked across the room. "The old guy!"

"That's him," Chatham said. "Like I said, an easy mark."

"Too easy," the skinhead allowed. "Maybe we should up the ante. He wants in," he said nodding at Kelly, "he's gotta knock off two Jews."

"No changing the rules," Chatham said, throwing his arm around Kelly's shoulder. "That one's enough."

Kelly turned an uneasy gaze back to the target, who was showing his ID to the guard. "Why him?"

The skinhead shook his head. "Here he goes again

with the questions. The kike's a traitor. You satisfied?"

"That's right," Chatham said, tightening his clasp of Kelly's shoulder. "He sold our military secrets to Israel. Unloaded a ton on them. And our friends, the Israelis, passed them on to the Soviets."

Kelly looked across the room again. The man was advancing through the line. "No shit? When was that?"

"About thirty years ago," Chatham said.

Frowning, Kelly asked, "Thirty years! So why's he getting it now?"

"Another fuckin' question," snarled the skinhead. "You got a problem with that?"

"No. No problem," Kelly said, shaking his head. "I was just wondering why now, is all."

"How 'bout that. He was just wonderin', is all," mimicked the skinhead.

"Because he wasn't going anywhere before," Chatham explained.

Kelly shot a look at his tormentor across the table before turning to Chatham. "And now he is?"

"Bastard's due for parole," Chatham said. "He should've been executed, but got life instead."

Kelly stole another glance at the mark, who had joined three others at their table. "They all Jews?"

"That's all he associates with," said Chatham. "But he's the only one claiming to be a political prisoner." Shaking his head, he said, "Can you beat that? He steals our secrets and then calls himself a political prisoner."

"Some pair of balls," Kelly said.

"You ask him, he'll say he had to do it because the Israelis live in a tough neighborhood and they need all the help they can get," Chatham said as he scooped up the last of his meal. "And since the U.S. wasn't doing enough, he was obliged to step up. He calls it *beshert*."

"*Besh* what?" Kelly said.

"It's Hebrew, for doing what you're destined to do," Chatham told him.

The skinhead grunted. "So now the fucker's destined to die."

"To show their gratitude," Chatham continued, "they made him a citizen and, if that wasn't enough, put him on the payroll. He's been collecting all these years."

"You sure know a lot about him," Kelly said.

"I make it a point to study a target before moving in," Chatham said with a wry smile. "Bastard's got a photographic memory, too."

"So?"

"So, he's got more secrets locked up in that miserable kosher head; secrets he'll pass to them once he's out."

The fourth man at the table, a muscular giant with ham hocks for fists, who Kelly knew only as Animal, and who'd been eating in silence, wiped the back of his hand across his mouth. "But you're gonna see he don't," he said, spraying bits of food across the table.

"Where?" Kelly asked. "Where am I gonna do it?"

"Outside," Chatham said. "We leave when he does," he said indicating the four of them. "We walk ahead of him, and Junior, here," he said nodding at the skinhead, "will be behind him. There's a blind spot out of view of the surveillance cameras beyond the second set of double doors. Usually, a guard's there, but there hasn't been one for several days. Part of the staff shortage I mentioned. That's where you get him."

"Get him with what? I still ain't got that shank."

"You will when it's time."

* * *

Twenty minutes later, Kelly and his tablemates rose and, disposing their trays and utensils in the rack by the door, exited the mess hall as Chatham had indicated.

"What about his pals?" Kelly whispered as they moved down the corridor. "They're witnesses."

"Don't worry," Chatham replied. "They know what happens to rats."

Voices in the narrow corridor echoed off the walls, growing louder as the mess hall emptied. With each step, the pill Kelly had taken earlier kicked in, easing his anxiety and diminishing his concern over the life he was about to terminate. Soon, he was feeling physically disconnected from the men around him.

Seeing the double doors ahead and no longer discerning Kleinman's voice behind him, he considered looking back to ensure his target was still within striking distance but, recalling Chatham's admonition about tells, suppressed the urge and continued on, his pace determined by the two men beside him. When Chatham spoke, telling him to get ready, his voice took on a peculiar distant quality, as if coming through a megaphone.

Passing through the double doors, Kelly saw the guard ahead and panicked, but when he blinked and looked again, there was no one. Ten feet beyond the double doors the shank was pressed into his hand and he was told, "Now!"

Kelly spun on command and saw the bearded traitor a few paces away conversing with friends. He hesitated. Again, the order. "Do it!" Raising his arm, he stepped forward and, shutting his eyes, drove the spike into the man's chest, imagining, as he did, the metal tip tearing into his victim's heart. In the next instant two strong hands whirled him around and propelled him forward while he attempted to blink the world back into focus. The cries for help rising behind him made him want to run, but the two men held him.

He was still gripping the shank when someone ordered, "Drop it!" He released his grip and continued walking, not feeling the ground beneath his feet or much of anything.

TWENTY-THREE

Do you believe her?" Sarah asked when we returned to the car.

I shrugged. "I'm not sure. She and her father certainly experienced enough grief to want to see Kleinman dead or harmed. Yet, she doesn't come across as the letter writer. There's something missing."

"What're you going to do?"

"Isn't much I can do."

"But she admitted mailing the letters!"

"Whoa. Take it easy. There are procedures..."

"Procedures? If she didn't write them she knows who did. Isn't that enough?"

"To do what?"

"To arrest her."

I was waiting for a break in traffic to pull out, and I shifted back into "park". Turning to her, I said, "Why are you so worked up all of a sudden? We'll get the information without the rubber hose approach. There are procedures to follow."

"And how long will that take?"

"A court order to put a tap on her phone and monitor her mail... A day or two."

"We don't have a day or two," she said, her voice

rising. "There's already been one attempt on his life."

"Sarah, I can't work outside the law."

"Well, I can!" she said. "She'll tell me who's writing those letters."

"What're you talking about?"

"I'm going in there and tell her she's under arrest."

"Forget it! You can't do that," I said, grabbing her arm.

"Goddamn it, Jerzy!" she said, tears welling in her eyes. "Why are you doing this to me?"

"What am I doing? I don't understand why you're so worked up over a lousy traitor."

"That traitor...," she said, looking back at the house.

"Yeah? What about him?"

Turning and taking my hand, she said, "Leo Kleinman's my husband."

I flinched. "WHAT?"

"He's my husband, and my name isn't Sarah Grayson. It's Ruth. Ruth Kleinman."

"You mean your brother. Kleinman's your brother."

"No. I don't have a brother, not in Butner or anywhere. The man I've been visiting is Leo Kleinman. The man you're trying to save. And if you don't do something, he may die."

"Jesus," I said shrinking into myself.

"Please, Jerzy, you have to understand."

I could barely hear her over the pounding in my ears. What was there to understand? I sat motionless behind the wheel staring at the woman I'd fallen for while she proceeded to tell me what I'd never imagined, and I certainly didn't want to hear.

"It was suggested that I... that we should meet. So I could monitor your progress."

I swallowed hard. "Monitor my progress? This has all been a goddamn charade? This thing between us?" I said, unable to suppress my anger.

She winced. "Not entirely."

"I'm confused. Help me understand which part is real?"

"The part about my wanting to be with you after our first meeting."

"Oh, the poor little prison widow found the sex pleasing. How comforting."

"You have every right to be angry. I'm truly sorry for misleading you. You don't deserve it. It wasn't my intention."

"And for that I should be grateful?"

She was shaking her head. "That isn't what I meant."

With my life veering off course, I looked at the woman who moments ago held center stage. Was she about to tell me she'd screwed up by not telling me sooner, and that she was now through with him? That it was over between them? This is how distorted my thoughts were at that moment. I'd accept any accommodation that set things straight between us. "What did you mean?" I asked with probably too much hope in my voice.

"My intent wasn't to hurt you. I was simply trying to help keep Leo safe."

Well, so much for that dream, I thought. "Is that it?" I said. And when the words I'd hoped to hear weren't forthcoming, I asked, "The encounter with that bozo at Pergamon, that was an act, too?"

She nodded.

"You two played your parts well. Must've had a good laugh between you. Who is he?"

"An associate of Max Goodman's."

"Ah. Dear old Max. I should've guessed he'd have a role in this. What's your connection to him? Please don't tell me he's your father."

"Just a friend."

"Just a friend?"

"Max represents certain foreign interests in this country."

"Come on, Sarah or Ruth. Whatever your name is. Don't be shy. Say it. He's connected to Israeli intelligence or the Mossad."

She shrugged. "It's possible. I really don't know. The Israelis have many friends in America, and many of them want to help Leo."

"So, it was Max, working with the Israelis, who put you on to me?"

"I was there the evening you two had dinner in Bethesda. He wanted me to see you."

"Of course, he did. Wanted to be sure you hooked the right fish at Pergamon. Max thinks of everything." My anger was returning.

She reached over, touching my arm. "Please. It isn't what it appears. There are many people who want Leo's sentence commuted so he can live what's left of his life in Israel, where he belongs. They've worked long and hard on his behalf. It may seem like they're conspiring against you, but they aren't."

I wanted to place my hand on hers, but I resisted. Instead, I said, "I guess that makes me a footnote in this saga."

Her eyes held mine, and she replied kindly. "Not to me, you aren't. I hadn't imagined anything would come of our meeting, but I was mistaken. It's been years since I've experienced such tenderness, such affection. You definitely lit a spark. It's been wonderful…"

I held my breath and thought, say it. Say, *I love you and I want to stay with you*. I was so desperate I'd have forgiven her if only she had said those words.

"…But I'm committed to Leo. I can't walk away now." She tightened her grip. "Please try to understand."

Understand? What did understanding have to do with anything? I had no interest in understanding. My world was crumbling. "We need to get to the hotel," I said, jerking my arm away and hitting the accelerator. "I have to get moving on Hattie Mullin if I'm going to save your husband."

The silence during our drive back weighed heavily on me, and I soon regretted my petulance. Several times I glanced over, but she never took her eyes from the road. There was no penetrating the wall that had come between us, not even back at the hotel, where I sat stiffly off to the side watching her pack.

The slow, methodical way she folded her clothes, had me thinking perhaps she wasn't anxious to leave after all. When she went to retrieve her toiletries from the bathroom I sprang up and quickly emptied her suitcase.

"What are you doing?" she asked when she returned.

I shrugged. "I don't know."

She looked at me and frowned.

"Don't go," I said.

"What's the point?"

I didn't have an answer. Instead, I watched her gather her clothes and shut her suitcase with a finality that made me shudder.

"I need to call a cab," she said after securing a seat on a flight to D.C. that evening.

"I'll drive you." And before she could decline, I quickly added, "Please."

"Okay," she said after a slight hesitation.

"This isn't how I imagined us parting," I said. She must have heard the pain in my voice. In the next instant, she was holding my face and gazing at me through teary eyes.

"You're a wonderful man, Jerzy Shore, and I care deeply for you. More than you realize." She kissed me tenderly, then pulled away. "If only there was some way of making this work."

I reached for her but she resisted. "Let's not make it more difficult than it is. We should be going," she said, retrieving her suitcase.

My cell phone rang. It was Theo.

"Great timing, Theo," I said forcing a cheerful voice.

"You with somebody?" he asked, his tone suggesting he meant a woman.

"No," I said, glancing at Sarah. I wanted her to be Sarah. I had fallen for Sarah, not Ruth. "What's up?"

"If you're driving, you may want to pull over." I told him I wasn't. "Good," he said. "You're off the case. In fact, the case is closed."

"What do you mean the case is closed?"

Sarah turned and froze.

"It's finito. Over. Shut down. There is no more case. There's been another attempt on the scumbag's life. A stabbing."

"Stabbing?" I said, immediately regretting it.

Sarah dropped her suitcase, and I said to Theo, "Hold on." Taking her arm, I steered her to a chair. "Stay calm," I told her with my hand over the phone. "He said *attempted* stabbing. Let me get the facts."

She nodded weakly.

"I'm back. What's this about?" I asked, eyeing Sarah, who had suddenly grown pale.

"Some clown tried stabbing him and got the guy next to him instead. But he was definitely aiming for Kleinman. At least, that's what the folks at Butner are telling us. They say it happened yesterday after dinner, outside the mess hall. The details are sketchy. We only just learned about it. Seems the guy went for Kleinman but he was too slow and Kleinman used another inmate as a shield, and that's who caught the knife."

"He's one lucky sonofabitch," I said, before holding my hand over the phone, and whispering, "He's all right. Another inmate got stabbed, not Leo." Then to Theo, I said, "So why's the case closed? Seems like it's hotter now."

"He's being moved out of Butner. Tomorrow the president will announce his commutation."

"You're joking!" Sarah was perched on the edge of her chair, leaning forward. I covered the phone again, and said, "He's coming out of Butner. Sentence is being commuted."

She clapped her hands, shouting, "Thank God!"

"Somebody there with you?" Theo asked.

"Just the TV."

"Anyway, it's no joke," Theo said. "This last attempt did it. They're advancing his parole date. From what we're hearing, the president doesn't want to piss off the Israelis. Better to give them a live hero than a dead one."

I looked at Sarah. She was crying.

"The chief wants you back ASAP. I'm guessing he doesn't want you eating up his travel budget."

When I finished with Theo, I turned to Sarah and said, "Looks like we'll be returning on the same flight."

* * *

Once she had calmed down, she phoned Max Goodman and learned Kleinman would be leaving Butner the following day; sometime prior to the president's announcement, thereby avoiding the media horde that was sure to swarm the prison. She was told he'd be traveling to Joint Base Andrews, outside D.C., via ConAir, where he'd be met by a delegation from the Israeli Embassy, and after being processed, would be free to proceed to Israel the next day.

With that bit of news, I argued there was no reason to rush back, urging her to consider returning to Washington with me the following day, and was relieved when she agreed.

The next morning, the sky was clear, a pale blue with puffs of clouds gathering on the horizon. We had left the sliding door ajar, and the breeze seeping in carried the scent of the river and the sound of early morning traffic. I eased out of bed, checking the time—we had till noon to catch our flight—and stepped outside. She was awake and sitting up when I returned.

"Good morning," she said stretching her arms above her head.

We began the previous evening agreeing the night was ours alone to enjoy, that tomorrow was too far away to think about. We joked it would be like Humphrey Bogart and Ingrid Bergman during their last night together in Paris in the film *Casablanca*. With that in mind, we set out to recapture magic moments, beginning with drinks at the Patterson House and dinner next door at the Catbird Seat, before strolling around the Parthenon, neither of us once mentioning what lay ahead for us after returning to Washington. Yet, despite our efforts, there was something missing or, more correctly, there was Leo Kleinman.

Now, kicking off the covers, she took me in her arms and opened herself to me. And unlike before, our movements were slow and gentle. And while I can't speak for Sarah, for my part, they were meant to keep my memory of her alive long after we separated. After taking our breakfast on the balcony, we headed to the airport, each of us lost in our thoughts.

"I'll miss you," I said as we taxied to the terminal in Washington.

"Me too," she replied, pressing her head into my

shoulder.

We walked to the cab stand, and embraced one last time. Her eyes, like mine, were moist when she broke away. Then, squeezing my arm, she smiled and, in her best Humphrey Bogart voice, said, "We'll always have Nashville."

I returned the smile and, closing the door to the taxi, said, "So long, kid."

My last view of Sarah—she would always be Sarah to me—was of her gazing at me and pressing her hand against the window as she rode away.

TWENTY-FOUR

This was Tom Kelly's first day out of solitary. Jailhouse lawyers had told him before he was placed in the special housing unit the feds had seven days to bring charges. This was the fourth day. Now, having been charged with attempted manslaughter, he stood before the warden for the first time since arriving at Butner, facing the man's unflinching stare. He was sandwiched between two correction officers, hands cuffed in front and secured to a thick leather belt cinched tight around his waist. The small, spotless office felt cramped with the four of them. Worse, it smelled of the same industrial disinfectant used in the units, but more pronounced in the confined space.

"Well, you've managed to screw up big time, Kelly. You turned a three-year sentence into a possible life sentence. Not very bright of you, son."

Kelly didn't respond. Instead his eyes remained fixed on the familiar item in the clear plastic evidence bag centered atop the warden's mahogany desk.

"To be blunt," the warden continued, "you're one dumb fucker."

The comment drew snickers from the two correction officers, causing Kelly to shift anxiously on his shackled feet.

"You got anything to say for yourself?" the warden asked.

"I'm innocent," he said, looking up at the warden, whose gunmetal gray hair blended with the dull sky behind him.

The warden nodded. "Of course you are. You and everyone else in this place."

Fellow inmates had advised Kelly to remain steadfast and not admit to anything. "Clam up," one had counseled. "Open your trap, and they'll use whatever you say against you."

The warden stood ramrod straight, meeting Kelly's gaze in silence until Kelly finally caved. "Why me? Why finger me for it?" he said, still trying to figure who had ratted him out.

"To begin with, your prints are all over this," he said, nodding at the shank sitting there between them.

Kelly shrugged. "That don't mean nothin'. I probably picked it up some place. I don't remember. It don't mean I was the one who used it."

"You mean someone tossed it after they stabbed the victim, and you found it?"

"Exactly! I found it in the yard, picked it up and tossed it so's I wouldn't get in trouble."

"Where'd you find it?"

He thought a moment. "Like I said, out in the yard. Over by the walking track. I didn't know what it was till I picked it up. Saw what it was and got rid of it pronto."

"Where? Where'd you toss it?"

"I, uh… In the bushes."

"Which bushes?"

Kelly shrugged. "How do I know? Bushes are bushes."

"You're going to need a better story."

"Why's that?"

"Because yours are the only prints." He let that sink in before adding, "Then, too, there's the problem of where we found it. I don't suppose you care to explain how it came to be taped to the underside of your locker?"

"Somebody put it there. I sure as hell didn't. I ain't that stupid."

"That's debatable. Any idea who put it there?"

Kelly shrugged his bony shoulders. "Could be anybody."

"How about your pals? Maybe one of them stashed it there?"

"No way. They'd never do that," he blurted before recalling Chatham's admonition about what happens to rats. "Besides, I got no pals."

"That isn't what I hear."

"I don't know what you're hearing. But it ain't right."

"According to your unit officer and unit manager, you've been associating with Lewis Chatham and his Aryan Brotherhood comrades. That's a tough group to be palling around with."

"Ain't no crime talking to people. A guy's got a right to talk to people."

"No, it isn't a crime. But attempted murder is."

Kelly's gaze fell to the dark green linoleum floor.

"How's it feel being their hand puppet?" the warden asked. And when Kelly didn't respond, he said, "Look at me, boy." Kelly raised his eyes. "You know you've been suckered? Your buddy Chatham and his pals used you."

"That's a lie! They wouldn't do that."

"They set you up for their own amusement, son. Played you like a piano."

"Nobody set me up."

"Then why'd you stab him? What did he do to you? I

bet you don't even know your victim's name."

"I didn't stab nobody."

The warden shook his head. "Guys like you never learn."

"I wasn't set up!" Kelly insisted, his voice growing more forceful. "They'd never do that."

"Who wouldn't do that? Chatham and his pals?"

Kelly licked his lips. "You're saying Chatham. I never said his name."

"That's who we're talking about."

Kelly shook his head. "I don't know who we're talking about. You're the one keeps throwing out names."

"They played you." And when Kelly didn't respond, "You remember how you got here? You were set up by some hoods from Atlantic City who turned on you. And now, you've been set up again. Folks see you coming a mile away. They feed you a line and you fall for it."

"That was different," Kelly replied. "They ratted me out to save their asses."

The warden sighed. "That may be, but you still got suckered, son, just like you've been suckered here by Chatham and his brothers."

"Bullshit! Nobody suckered me."

"Watch your language, kid," the CO to his left said, delivering a jab below his ribs that buckled Kelly and had him gasping.

"You weren't their first sucker and you sure as hell won't be the last," the warden said.

When Kelly regained his breath he shot the guard a dirty look. "Tough guy. Like to see you do that when I ain't shackled."

"How about me?" his partner said, landing a second blow that dropped Kelly to his knees. "Care to square off with me, wise guy?"

The three men stood silent while Kelly unfolded

himself.

"Are we finished?" he said, his color drained from his face.

"We're finished when I say we're finished," the warden told him. After a long silence, he said, "I'm going to do you a favor because you're young and, from the looks of it, you're going to be in the system a long time. Gonna tell you how you got suckered, and maybe you'll learn something.

"Whatever."

Ignoring the remark, the warden said, "They come when you're most vulnerable, real friendly-like. Usually a week or two after you arrive, while you're in the holding area and don't know anyone. They get you talking about yourself and sympathize with you. Tell you they know being a newbie's tough. What they don't tell you is it gets tougher when guys see you warming up to them, guys who don't cotton to that group and who don't mind kicking your ass."

"That ain't true," Kelly protested. "I fell those times."

"Sure you did. That's what they all tell the doc if they know what's good for them," the warden said. "One day they step up and help get you transferred out of the holding area into a friendlier unit. Sound familiar?"

Kelly didn't reply.

"It's the same routine every time. The only thing that changes is the target. Next, you're eating with them in the mess hall, working out with them in the gym, and watching television like one happy family. All very comfy-cozy."

"So what's wrong with that?" Kelly said.

"What's wrong? They isolated you from the rest of the population is what's wrong, if you haven't already figured it out," the warden replied. "Other inmates see this and they steer clear of you. No one wants to mess with the Brotherhood. And when they suggest joining up—becoming one of them—you agree because you know what'll happen if you don't. But first, you have to demonstrate your loyalty, they tell you."

Kelly was twisting his jaw and looking intently at the warden now.

"Becoming a member requires killing someone. But don't worry, they say, we'll help you. All you have to do is stick the bastard. Sound about right?"

Kelly held his silence.

"They picked a nice victim for you—Kleinman, the traitor. The one everyone here loves to hate. No doubt they gave you this," he said, nodding at the evidence bag. "Funny how someone can pass a weapon without leaving his prints on it. And then… Well, we know what happened next. You did everything asked of you, except one thing." His lips curled into an ugly grin. "You stabbed the wrong Yid."

There was an uncomfortable silence while what little confidence Kelly had left leached from him.

"They hooked you. Then they reeled you in," the warden said.

Kelly swallowed hard.

"Oh, about the shank. I'll bet one of your pals grabbed it after you used it. Probably the same one who planted it where we found it."

"I don't know what you're talking about," Kelly said without conviction.

The warden shook his head. "You're going back to the SHU for your own protection. Soon you'll be transferred to another facility. Once you're indicted, the prosecutor will likely offer you an opportunity to plead to a lesser offense. If you're smart, take it. Probably only get ten years, eight with good behavior. All you'll have to do is ID the men who put you up to this."

Kelly didn't respond.

The warden nodded at the guards. Kelly's tutorial was over. They spun him around and marched him toward the door. From behind, the warden tossed out one final piece of wisdom. "No matter where you land, son. Remember. You have no friends in prison."

TWENTY-FIVE

One morning not long afterward, while returning to my office from a staff meeting, I heard Theo call out as I shuffled past his door.

"Qué pasa, Iceman?"

"Not much," I replied, and continued on, preferring to be alone.

"Hold on, a sec, big fella," he shouted, calling me back. He studied me a moment as I stood in his doorway. "You still down about that oddball Kleinman case?"

I didn't say what was on my mind, which was Sarah. Instead, I said, "It would've been satisfying to have tracked down the letter writer."

"You were getting close. If they hadn't freed the traitor and pulled you back here, you would have."

I appreciated the uplifting thought. "Thanks," I said with a forced smile. "She appeared to be an interesting character. I would've liked hearing her side of the story."

Theo said what we both knew. "She did a nice job of poisoning the well down there at Butner. She was one determined gal."

"Not determined," I said. She was obsessed."

Once again I found myself wishing one of Kleinman's attackers had succeeded and made Sarah a widow.

"I wonder how she's handling it," Theo was saying.

"Who?"

"The gal who wrote the letters," he said. "I wonder how she's handling Kleinman's release. Too bad you couldn't shake it out of that Hattie Mullin gal. Get her to ID the woman."

Hearing Hattie Mullin's name pulled me back to the day Sarah broke the news about being Kleinman's wife. It wasn't something I wanted to dwell on, and I said, "Yeah, well… it's history. Time to move on," and started for my office.

"Cheer up!" he called. "Brighter days are ahead."

Yeah. Brighter days. I was ready for them. I had lost count of the times I'd rearranged my furniture and feng shui ornaments here and at home, hoping to recapture the positive chi that seemed to have evaporated of late. Something had to change, and thankfully it did a few days later. Perhaps it was the chi after all.

The unexpected phone call came late one evening. I didn't recognize the name Deidra Thomas on my Caller ID, and I answered thinking she was connected to my current case. It happened often that way, tips from callers at odd hours, when they felt it was safe to call; safe for them.

"This is Agent Shore," I said into the phone.

"I've decided to see if you're man enough for me." The voice was throaty and vaguely familiar.

"Who is this?"

"You don't remember me?" She sounded offended.

"Well… I…"

"Hmmm. I thought you would," she said, before reminding me we had met months earlier at the speed dating party with the Hawaiian theme.

I was trying to put a face to the name, when she said, "Meet anyone particularly interesting that night?

Someone you kept looking at after you moved on to the other tables? You didn't think I noticed."

I crossed the living room and settled into my chair. Of course, I thought, propping my feet on the coffee table. The tattooed lady with the penetrating eyes. I had hoped she'd contact me afterward, and then forgotten her when she hadn't.

"Now that you mention it," I said, "there was this enchanting woman sporting a rather colorful dragon tattoo."

"Well, here I am," she chimed, and at that moment I felt the positive chi flowing around me again.

TWENTY-SIX

The postcard arrived at Hattie Mullin's home one afternoon, nearly five weeks to the day since the two NCIS agents appeared at her door inquiring about the letters she had forwarded to Kleinman at Butner. She carried it with her to the rear porch after placing the rest of the mail on the dining room table, now clear of her father's meds. There, Hattie stretched out on the divan and, lowering her eye glasses from her forehead, read the penned message.

> *Dearest Hattie,*
>
> *Enjoying sunny Tel Aviv. Friendly people. Wonderful food. Found small apartment and have settled in. Don't know for how long. Depends!!! Writing this from lovely café on beautiful Rothschild Blvd. (see photo opposite side) within walking distance of K's place. Looking forward to closing that circle. Hope you are well.*
>
> *Love, Laura*

Hattie smiled and, pushing her glasses up again, closed her eyes and dozed off, the postcard slipping from her hand.

TWENTY-SEVEN

How best to describe Deidra Thomas? After several dates, I concluded she was right when cautioning me at our first meeting that she was more woman than I could handle.

It wasn't the pace of our dates that wore me down, or the sleek sex. It was the mental games she enjoyed playing; not just with me, but with everyone we encountered. Craving the spotlight, she'd enter a room and within minutes hijack conversations. Oddly, she always pulled it off in a way that was neither crass nor offensive, not even when issuing commands to strangers who seemed more than willing to obey them. More off-putting were the times we were alone together. Sometimes, without warning, she'd retreat into a shell and resist all attempts to draw her out. Other times, she might morph into a shy, obsequious school girl or a Chatty Cathy or a saucy minx. It got so, I never knew who would greet me at the door when I came for her, or who I'd end the night with. I had never known anyone like Deidra.

Still, I tolerated her antics. She was intelligent and remarkably engaging, providing a spontaneity that enabled me to get on with my life after Sarah. And though

I knew it couldn't last—nothing could at that pace—it came as a surprise when it did. We were returning from a long weekend on Maryland's Eastern Shore. She had grown silent as we drove and, sensing something was bothering her, I inquired and was calmly informed the zest was gone between us and it was time to call it quits. I said I was surprised she felt that way, but since she did, we might want to talk about it, but she declined. And that was that, another abrupt breakup.

It was about that time I received another unexpected call.

"Jerzy, it's Max Goodman. How are you?" His enthusiasm threw me, and before I could reply, he said, "It's time we had a meal together."

My anger at being played by him returned, and I said, "Why? You planning to set me up again?"

"Don't talk foolish," he said.

"You played me, Max. Played me like a piano."

"What do I know from pianos? I'm calling to invite you to sit down and share a meal with me."

"The case is closed, Max. Your boy is in Israel where you wanted him. What's the point?"

"The point is, I'm an old man and I want to see you."

"I can't imagine why," I said.

"Does there have to be a grand plan? Come have dinner with me. We'll share a *bissel* wine, have a nice meal and we'll talk. Is that so difficult?" When I hesitated, "Can't you do me this tiny favor?"

I sighed. The guy was incorrigible. "All right, Max. But spare me the old man line."

"You're a sweetheart. How's tomorrow?"

"Tomorrow?"

"You have something more important?"

"No, Max. Tomorrow's fine. Same place? Morton's in Bethesda?"

"Perfect," he said. "See you at six thirty."

The call left me thinking of Sarah, of how she had colluded with him—lingering in the shadows, sizing me up, while Max and I dined. It wasn't a pleasant thought and I didn't know if I should be angry with her or him, or both of them. The truth is, I couldn't be angry with her. As for Max, well…

The same elderly maître d' greeted me, before leading me across the room to Goodman's table, where he pulled out my chair, then withdrew after unfurling my napkin and handing it to me. As before, there was an open bottle of Pinot Noir, two half-filled wine glasses and a chilled bottle of Perrier. The man was consistent, I'd give him that.

As I expected, he was impeccably dressed. His hair was neatly trimmed and his bright eyes alert and shining. "Good to see you. You look splendid," he said with that winning smile while rising slightly from his chair and extending his manicured hand.

I returned the greeting, thinking, how could anyone not like this fellow?

Once seated, he motioned to the wine. "I remembered that you like this one." Then, lifting his glass, he said, "To friends."

Not for a second did I believe he considered me a friend. Still, I echoed the sentiment. "To friends."

It wasn't until after dinner, when the table had been cleared, that he mentioned Kleinman.

"We appreciate your efforts on Leo's behalf," he said. "You did your best under difficult circumstances. Like trying to find a needle in a haystack."

The reference to *we* rankled me, because I knew he was alluding to Kleinman's supporters here and abroad, people who approved of his betrayal or aided him in his thefts. Since there was nothing to be gained going over that old ground, I simply replied, "I was doing my job."

"And for that you have our gratitude."

"I would've felt better had I identified the letter writer," I said, rather than telling him what I was really thinking. That I didn't give a damn about their gratitude and, as far as I was concerned, anyone associated with Kleinman was no better than he was.

"From what I heard, you would have found her given a little more time."

"From what you heard… You're referring to your spy."

His smile melted, and shaking his head, he said, "That's a harsh term—spy. We had to know what was happening. What was being done to protect Leo. I'm sure you can understand."

"I understand perfectly, Max. You used me," I said without rancor. "It's that simple. Can we at least agree on that?"

He shrugged. "I repeat. It was necessary."

"Is that why you invited me here? To tell me it was necessary?"

"Partly. And to give you this," he said, taking an envelope from his jacket and sliding it across to me. "She asked me to deliver it personally. Now, if you'll excuse me," he said, rising. "I must visit the restroom."

Max's gesture of granting me some privacy was appreciated. The envelope—sealed and bearing no inscription—remained untouched while he exited the room. Part of me wanted to tear it open, hoping the message inside was alerting me of her imminent return. Instead, I took a long sip of wine before reaching for it. Then, easing open the flap, I read Sarah's handwritten note.

Dear Jerzy,

I hope this finds you well. By now, you must be working

hard on another case. We are settled in Tel Aviv, in a lovely apartment overlooking the Jaffa promenade and the beautiful Mediterranean beyond. Leo is happy, which makes me happy. I think of you often and of our time together. You are a very special man and you shall always hold a dear place in my heart. This will be the last time I reach out to you. I pray you find the woman you deserve.

With deep affection,

R

Max returned while I was reading it for the third or fourth time, our waiter close by, ready to assist him with his chair.

"Thank you," I said, folding the note and pocketing it.

He offered a tender smile. "Don't be angry with her. If you must, be angry with me."

"I'm not angry with anyone."

"Good. Let it be so." With a wink, he added, "You're what we call a *haimisher mensch*, Jerzy." Noting my frown, he said, "It's a compliment!"

When I stood to leave, he clasped my hand and said, "Leo's where he belongs. He's with his people, where he'll be safe."

TWENTY-EIGHT

Laura's life in Tel Aviv took on the slow rhythm of the eastern Mediterranean climate and its people. Though embarked on a mission, she no longer felt compelled to act. She could move at her own pace without fretting over the actions or inactions of others, as she had at Butner. From all appearances, Kleinman wasn't going anywhere anytime soon, which meant neither was she. Having her mark within easy reach, allowed her to savor her options. She could strike when and how she wanted. And with that knowledge came a serenity that banished the nightmares and mood swings that had plagued her.

In stalking her quarry, Laura's days followed Kleinman's, whose unremarkable lifestyle mirrored the same unswerving routine he had grown accustomed to during thirty years of incarceration. Each morning, he'd leave his apartment at the same time, wearing slight variations of what she came to think of as his uniform—pressed khaki pants, sandals and flowered shirts. Taking the same route, he'd walk along tony Sderot-Rothschild Boulevard, known as White City because of the sleek uniformity of its white buildings, and appear at the same seafront restaurant, the one overlooking Alma

Beach and the ancient port of Old Jaffa, shortly before it opened, where he'd take the same table and order fried eggs, toast, salad and hummus. When the dishes were removed, he'd immerse himself in the *Jerusalem Post* for the next hour before walking the half mile or so to the sprawling Jaffa flea market on Yehuda Margoza and Beit Eshel Streets. There, he'd stroll the narrow aisles and haggle with vendors and peddlers over such ordinary items as ornate picture frames, colorful Indian pillow covers, Judaica items, kitchenware, scarves, shirts or anything else that caught his eye. Here, too, the procedure didn't vary. Having selected an object, he'd engage the vendor for several minutes, replace the item, leave and circle the market before returning to close the deal. On one occasion, she observed him leave a stall and return several times before finally purchasing what looked to be a centuries-old carved door knocker. Hardly a day passed without a purchase, revealing post-prison eccentricities of interacting with people only on his terms and acquiring objects, no matter how unnecessary or impractical.

On the rare days his wife accompanied him to breakfast, Laura was surprised at how disconnected and mismatched the couple were. From her vantage point, they appeared to be strangers—the woman sipping her coffee in silence and gazing at the parade of sunbathers and bicyclists, while Kleinman shoveled down his breakfast. It was only when he unfolded his newspaper that she seemed to acknowledge him. Standing and straightening her skirt, she would bend at the waist and plant a kiss on his forehead, as a parent does when sending a child off to school, and then depart. For whatever reason, she never accompanied him to the flea market.

Curious, Laura followed the woman on several

occasions, certain this stunning beauty was meeting a lover, someone more suited to her than the frumpy, overweight Kleinman. But there was no one, at least not on the days Laura observed her.

The woman's routine was as constant as her husband's. After leaving the restaurant, she would stroll west to the Suzanne Dellal Center, a sprawling campus for distinguished dance troupes. There, she would enter the interior court yard, select one of the unoccupied benches beside the gurgling irrigation canals, and spend her time reading beneath the citrus trees. Around noon, she'd close her book and lunch at one of the coffee houses in nearby Neve Tzekek district before visiting the area's high fashion boutiques. And though many men smiled at her or tried to engage her, she never responded or appeared to encourage them.

The only change in the couple's routine that Laura detected, aside from occasional day trips to Jerusalem, occurred on Saturdays when they dined at a pedestrian restaurant in City Center, rather than the upscale one run by Meir Adoni, one of Israel's bright young chefs, which they frequented. Laura guessed they opted for the change because they sought the company of American expatriates who gathered there on weekends. It was there, early one Saturday evening, that she decided to initiate her plan. Sidling up to the couple's table she asked if she might join them, explaining how thrilled she was to meet a true Israeli hero. The meeting went well, and two days later she feigned surprise when running into Kleinman at the Jaffa flea market.

"What a wonderful coincidence," she exclaimed.

"I was thinking the same thing," he said with a warm smile. "What brings you here?"

She said she'd heard about the wide selection of merchandise and bargains, telling him she enjoyed browsing the stalls and searching for antiques.

"You should come on Fridays," he said, "when anyone who can find room to spread a blanket is welcome to sell their wares."

She was holding a small bag of dried apricots. "They're delicious," she said, offering them.

After a few minutes, he suggested stopping for coffee. She agreed and, taking his arm, allowed him to steer her through the narrow walkways to a nearby stand. Afterward, they walked the market together while he shared tips on how to haggle with vendors. Before parting, they agreed to meet the following day. By week's end, he was literally eating out of her hand — consuming chocolates, nuts, figs, olives—whatever she offered him. He'd dip his pudgy hand into the bag, grab whatever was there and shove a handful in his mouth while she smiled inwardly.

Poisoning Kleinman was going to be easy.

TWENTY-NINE

I was reviewing a cold case file, hoping to uncover a new lead, when Scully popped into my office unexpectedly, sporting a sly grin, which was rare for him. "You'll never guess what happened," he said, dropping into the chair across from me. Without waiting for a response, he continued, "They got a set of prints from the letter."

"Letter? What letter?" I said.

"One of the anonymous letters that loony woman sent to Kleinman down in Butner. FBI lab retrieved a good set of prints."

I shook my head. "How's that possible? They went through dozens of hands."

"I'm not talking about the ones you got from that Goodman guy. You're right, they were useless. This one arrived at Butner *after* Kleinman left. So he never got to open it. That gal in Nashville…"

"Hattie Mullin," I said.

"Yeah, that one. Must've dropped it in the mail after he was transferred out. Can you beat that?"

"The Lord works in mysterious ways. Still, how'd they pull useful prints after it went through the prison mailroom?"

"That's just it," Scully said. "Because Kleinman was

gone they sent it straight to the warden unopened. He forwarded it up the chain, and they passed it to the FBI. *They* opened it."

He was clearly enjoying himself, and I was tempted to tell him about the positive chi flowing around us, but that would only spoil things. Instead, I asked, "And now you're going to tell me they were able to ID the writer?" I was having trouble wrapping my head around this unforeseen twist in my case.

The grin was now a broad smile. "Yep. Ran the prints through the national data base and got a match. They're in the system because she's a BOP employee. Name's Laura Greene. A dental hygienist who transferred to Butner from Schuylkill."

Now I couldn't help smiling. My thoughts went to Nashville, and I said, "God bless Hattie. So, I was right. The writer, this Laura Greene, was inside."

"Not the whole time," Scully said. "Looks like she started her letter campaign while at Schuylkill and when that didn't pan out, she transferred to Butner to get close to Kleinman."

"She probably had something to do with those two attempts," I said. "They pick her up?"

Scully shook his head. "She bailed. Quit after Kleinman went free."

"Do we know where she is?"

The sly grin returned. "You're gonna love this. She hasn't given up. The crazy woman's on a mission. She's in Israel. Her name popped up in TSA's files when the feds did a search."

That's when he hit me with the bombshell.

"How'd you like to bring her back?"

* * *

Less than twenty-four hours later I was standing outside Leo Kleinman's third floor apartment in one of Tel Aviv's premier residential districts, steeling myself to face the woman I couldn't shake from my mind, should my wish be granted and she answer my knock.

I heard footsteps inside, light footsteps against the marble floor, and I took a deep breath and steadied myself. Every fiber in my body was alive. The door opened, and she gasped.

She looked fantastic.

"Hi," I said. "It's been a while." I was struggling to appear calm, but the crack in my voice wasn't helping. Fortunately, she was as unprepared as I and didn't seem to notice.

She swallowed hard and said, "Wha… what are you doing here?"

"I couldn't keep away."

"I don't believe this." She was gripping the door as though she might collapse without it. Blinking away tears, she said, "I can't tell you how often I've thought of you."

"Well, here I am. Are you going to invite me in?"

She took my arm and pulled me inside, closing the door behind me. We were inches apart in the narrow entryway. Not knowing if we were alone, I stood there wanting to take this radiant, sun-tanned beauty in my arms, but holding back fearing Kleinman might appear any second. I needn't have worried. The way she threw her arms around my neck and kissed me—a tender, unhurried kiss—told me there was nothing to fear.

"God, I missed you," I said.

"Me too," she said, pressing into me.

"But I missed you more."

"Be quiet, you silly man," she replied, sounding like a giddy school girl, "and kiss me. And don't stop."

I didn't need prompting, and we continued like that for some time. Until she finally asked, "Why didn't you tell me you were coming?"

"I didn't know till yesterday," I said, letting her lead me into a well-appointed living room with a spectacular view of the blue sea stretching to the cloudless horizon.

We fell onto the sofa, she in my lap, her arms tight around my neck, mine around her waist, neither of us wanting to let go. The open patio doors invited a cool breeze that played against her perfumed skin and brushed her silky hair against my face. It was an intoxicating moment. How often I had dreamed of holding her like this, and how I hated for it to end. But it did, when she finally got around to asking why I had come.

I wanted to say I'd come to take her away, back to America with me. It seemed so natural with her there in my arms. In that brief instant I believed she might have agreed. But, of course, that didn't happen. Poor Sarah. One moment she was flying high and the next, her world was shattered, as I explained what had brought me to Israel. "She's here?" she said, sliding off my lap, her voice trembling. I nodded, and she asked, "How long?"

"She left the States several weeks ago."

"No. It can't be," she said shaking her head and drawing into herself. And when I didn't respond, there was a pleading in her voice. "Are you sure? Could there be some mistake?"

"No mistake. She flew directly here and hasn't re-entered the U.S.," I said handing her the photo Scully had given me. "Her name's Laura Greene. Have you seen her?"

"I thought we were safe." Then, creasing her brow, she studied the expressionless woman with mousey shoulder-length hair and no makeup. "We meet so many Americans. Is this a recent photo?"

"It was taken about ten years ago. We pulled it from her personnel file."

"And the name. You said…"

"Laura Greene."

She pursed her lips. "There was a woman. An American. Could be her. But the name was different."

"Probably changed it, as well as her appearance," I said.

Her eyes returned to the photo. "Prettier. Shorter hair. Almost butch, and lighter. Approached us a week or so ago. Said she recognized Leo. All bubbly and excited about meeting him. Calling him a patriot and a hero. But then, lots of folks do that here. They just stop us on the street and tell him how brave he was. A real mensch."

"And the name?" I said.

She was tapping the photo against her knee. "Her name?" After a moment, she said, "I want to say Ellen. No not Ellen. Liz. I'm pretty sure it was Liz." Another pause, and a nod. "Liz Ross. That was it. Said her friends call her Betty, but she preferred Liz. From Pennsylvania, I think."

I couldn't help myself, and when I laughed I was greeted with a stern look.

"What's so funny?"

"Could she have said Philadelphia?"

Sarah's jaw dropped. "Yes! Philadelphia. How'd you know?"

I sighed. "Liz. Elizabeth Ross from Philadelphia…" I said, and paused. Getting a blank expression, I said, "The Liberty Bell…"

"I'm not following you," she said with a touch of pique.

"Liz, like Betty, is short for Elizabeth. So is Betsy.

Betsy Ross. The USS *Liberty*."

"My god. How stupid of us!"

"Not stupid, just trusting. There'd be no reason for you to suspect her, or make that connection sitting here, six thousand miles away? She was toying with you."

"Like a cat toys with a mouse," she said. "We were careless. We should've been more mindful."

"I don't know. This is a pretty spectacular city you're living in. I can see how you could let your guard down. Has she been in touch since then?"

"No. We haven't seen or heard from her. Americans come and go." Her eyes widened. "But she hasn't gone. She's still here."

"Looks that way."

Jumping up, she said, "We've got to find Leo!"

How ironic, I thought. Here we are working the case together again. "Where is he?"

She glanced at her watch. "He should be at the flea market." Taking my hand, she pulled me up. "We have to go."

Once outside, she hit the sidewalk running and continued into the street, where she was nearly hit flagging down a taxi.

"You don't have a car?"

"We don't drive," she said, yanking open the door with a force that nearly unhinged it. "It's easier this way."

We hopped in and she told the driver, "Jaffa flea market. Hurry!"

"Is it far?" I asked, as he accelerated.

"No. We usually walk." We entered a traffic circle and she pointed to an old limestone clock tower ahead of us. "It's just beyond the tower."

Moments later, we were swerving onto a narrow street. When the driver slowed, Sarah tapped his shoulder and said something in Hebrew or Yiddish that had him leaning on the horn, scattering bicyclists and pedestrians. We took another hard turn and went about fifty feet before making an abrupt stop.

"This is it," she said, withdrawing some bills from her purse and throwing them across the front seat.

"Where do we begin?" I said, jumping out behind her.

She stood on the crowded sidewalk shaking her head. "I wish I knew."

* * *

Laura, meanwhile, was deep inside the market standing beside a spice shop where she'd agreed to meet Kleinman. She was rocking on her heels and wiping her sweaty palms on her dress, signs he was sure to detect if she didn't calm herself. She had grown increasingly anxious since their first meeting, but not because of any reservations about killing him. That hadn't changed. What troubled her was that she kept putting it off. To her surprise, she was enjoying his company—the little traitor, she discovered, could be quite charming and endearing. For the past several days she'd been carrying two bags of sweets—Turkish Delights, his favorites— one laced with poison. However, each time she reached into her handbag, she'd bring out the untainted variety.

Now, after a fitful night, she had made up her mind. Today, she would do what she had come here to do. There would be no more delays. The poison she carried to Israel—methylmorphine, commonly known as codeine, a powdery, transparent and odorless analgesic that suppresses the central nervous system—was difficult to detect and highly toxic, but she hadn't chosen it solely for those reasons. She chose it because death would be slow and painful. Certainly, not as horrible as what the Israeli rockets and napalm had inflicted on her uncle's shipmates, or as slow as he and many other injured survivors had endured over the years. But then, it wasn't a perfect world. Considering Kleinman's age and girth, she estimated he'd succumb in an hour, two at most, as his heartbeat slowed and his lungs filled with fluid. That, she reasoned, would allow ample time to tell him who she really was and why she had come for him. It was important that he know that.

"There you are," he called as he came around the corner. He was right on time.

They hugged and she slipped her arm around his.

* * *

I found the massive indoor bazaar overwhelming. Narrow alleys barely wide enough for two and teeming with merchants, stretching out in every direction beneath a covered arcade, where rows of ceiling fans added to the noise level. Wasting little time, Sarah grabbed my hand and pulled me down an aisle of stalls, each crammed with merchandise. There were oriental carpets, bolts upon bolts of cloth in various colors and fabrics, brassware, cut glass, kitchenware, jewelry, loads of jewelry, and vendors of every stripe beckoning us with raised voices in unfamiliar languages. The deeper we ventured into this labyrinth the less confident I became of finding Kleinman. Sarah, however, remained focused. Gripping my hand tightly, she pressed forward, propelling us through knots of shoppers and sightseers.

Where aisles intersected, she pivoted left and then left again at the next intersection, and I soon understood we were crisscrossing the market in an orderly grid.

"He's got to be here somewhere," she kept mumbling.

"Got to be."

I had nothing to add and simply kept pace with her. Several times she stopped, pulling me up short, only to realize the man she'd seen wasn't Kleinman.

* * *

Laura had admired Kleinman's sandals, and now she was about to have a pair of her own. She was seated cross-legged on a low stool in the cramped shoemaker's stall allowing him to fit her with a pair similar to Kleinman's, her skirt hiked to her thighs. When she looked up and winked at Kleinman, who was leaning against the wall popping Turkish Delights in his mouth, barely swallowing one before reaching for another, he grinned like a Cheshire cat.

They had stopped on the way for coffee and a croissant, a few crumbs still clinging to his beard after she had brushed most of them away. The café was small, no tables, just a standup bar, the crush of patrons forcing them together, close enough for her to feel his erection, which prompted her to press in and twist her hips, and him to cup her breast and offer a slight squeeze.

And though the encounter passed without comment, it ignited a passion in Kleinman that hadn't been there before; a passion revealed in hungry looks when gazing at her, as he was doing now, and which she returned in a manner that kept him hopeful and off balance.

* * *

I'm fairly certain we spotted him at the same time. He was about thirty feet away, his attention directed into the shop and the woman seated there. But it was Sarah who sprinted ahead.

"Leo!" she called.

He turned, and there was no mistaking his resentment at the intrusion, causing her to pause. As I ran past her, the woman came into view, and I shouted, "Laura Greene!"

In that instant, it was clear from Kleinman's expression he recognized me. A quick look back at Greene, whose face had turned hard and ugly, told him all he needed to know. Dropping the bag, he began spitting out what he'd been chewing and using his fingers to pry away what remained, all this while Sarah rushed forward and pushed him away. I, in turn, shoved the shopkeeper aside and lunged for Laura Greene, but not before the small caliber gun she withdrew from her handbag exploded in the cramped space. I grabbed her hand and twisted it back before she could fire another round. Undeterred, she began clawing my face with her free hand while letting loose a stream of obscenities. Her grip was strong, and when the gun finally fell I slammed my fist into her jaw and she crumbled. It was then, with Laura lying unconscious beneath me, that I turned to see Sarah atop Kleinman, blood oozing from the base of her skull.

Sarah died instantly. Not so Kleinman, who, they tell me, slipped in and out of consciousness after arriving at the hospital. It was not a peaceful death, they said.

Later, working through the American Embassy in Tel Aviv, I briefed the national police at their headquarters in Jerusalem, outlining Laura Greene's crusade to avenge Israel's attack on the *Liberty* by assassinating one of their country's modern-day heroes, my role in discovering her identity and my attempts at preventing her from doing so.

I needn't have bothered. Much of what I told them they already knew, including Hattie Mullin's identity.

They were also quick to iterate the government's long-held stance that the two-hour aerial and torpedo attack on the ship during the Six Day War had been an unfortunate accident for which the government had already apologized and paid reparation. Sadly, I detected no remorse. Our subsequent request to extradite Laura Greene to the United States was denied without benefit of an official hearing, the government asserting jurisdiction because she had murdered two of its citizens on Israeli soil.

I stayed for the funeral, watching as Kleinman was given full military honors that included the Chief of Staff of the Israel Defense Forces placing an Israeli national flag on his grave. It was a moving ceremony that took place on a cloudless morning at Mount Herzl National Cemetery in western Jerusalem, where Kleinman was interred among Zionist leaders, Israeli heroes and Holocaust and terrorist victims, Sarah beside him. Standing there on the fringe of the crowd, a gentle breeze brushing my face, I wondered how things might've turned out had I reached Laura Greene a split-second sooner. With Kleinman dead, would Sarah have returned to America? And might we have forged a life together? Was I being foolish? I thought not. Until Scully had dispatched me to bring Laura Greene back, the possibility of seeing Sarah again was as remote as a distant star. Yet, less than twenty-four hours later, we were in each other's arms. It seemed, given this second chance, we were destined for each other.

When the crowd dispersed, I moved forward, and as I gazed down at their graves I was forced to admit she would never have been mine. She belonged to Kleinman, and always had.

ACKNOWLEDGEMENTS

As with any novel, there are numerous people who contribute to the final opus. In this instance, I have relied on members of my writers group for their comments and suggestions. Fortunately for me, all are dedicated to improving the writing craft. My thanks to each of you.

I appreciate the assistance of retired FBI Special Agent Sharon S. Smith, Ph.D., in helping me understand the complex field of psycholinguistics. Thanks, too, to my longtime friend Colonel Lou Cherico, USMC (Ret.) for his valuable assistance and guidance, without which this book might not have progressed much beyond the first chapter. Likewise, I wish to thank James M. Ennes, Jr., for directing me to his riveting work, *Assault on the Liberty*, a must read for anyone interested in learning the details of that horrific day. And once again, I extend my appreciation to Ed Jaffee for his willingness to be a second set of eyes in the proofreading phase. To Melanie Stephens, of MS Illustration and Design, Fredericksburg, VA, you are a professional in every sense of the word. Thank you for your sound advice and for applying your exceptional skills in laying out the book and designing the cover.

ABOUT THE AUTHOR

George Vercessi is a retired U.S. Navy captain residing in Virginia. He is the author of five previous novels, an illustrated children's Christmas tale and a guide for authors wishing to self-publish, as well as developing and co-producing the MGM/Showtime drama *The Silver Strand*, featuring Nicolette Sheridan and Gil Bellows.

For additional information please visit
www.vercessi.com.